CAN'T BUY ME LOVE

BUTLER, VERMONT SERIES, BOOK 2

MARIE FORCE

Can't Buy Me Love
Butler, Vermont Series, Book 2
By: Marie Force

Published by HTJB, Inc.
Copyright 2017. HTJB, Inc.
Cover Design: Ashley Lopez
Print Layout: E-book Formatting Fairies
ISBN: 978-1946136664

**The Green Mountain and
Butler, Vermont Series**

The Green Mountain Series
Book 1: All You Need Is Love *(Will & Cameron)*
Book 2: I Want to Hold Your Hand *(Nolan & Hannah)*
Book 3: I Saw Her Standing There *(Colton & Lucy)*
Book 4: And I Love Her *(Hunter & Megan)*
Novella: You'll Be Mine *(Will & Cam's Wedding)*
Book 5: It's Only Love *(Gavin & Ella)*
Book 6: Ain't She Sweet *(Tyler & Charlotte)*

The Butler, Vermont Series
(Continuation of Green Mountain)
Book 1: Every Little Thing *(Grayson & Emma)*
Book 2: Can't Buy Me Love *(Mary & Patrick)*
Book 3: Here Comes the Sun *(Wade & Mia)*
Book 4: Till There Was You *(Lucas & Dani)*
Book 5: All My Loving *(Landon & Amanda)*
Book 6: Let It Be *(Lincoln & Molly)*
Book 7: Come Together *(Noah & Brianna)*

More new books are always in the works. For the most up-to-date list of what's available from the Butler, Vermont Series as well as series extras, go to *marieforce.com/vermont*

CHAPTER 1

"Do you want to be safe and good,
or do you want to take a chance and be great?"
—Jimmy Johnson

*H*e'd sent a car for her. The concept, when he first mentioned it, was so foreign to her as to be baffling. Why did she need someone to drive her when she was perfectly capable of driving herself? But he'd insisted, and now that the appointed day had arrived, Mary was thankful she didn't have to drive across the state. She was far too nervous to drive two hours to meet the first man who'd sparked her interest in years.

And he wasn't just any man. No, this was Patrick Murphy, *the* Patrick Murphy, as in the billionaire businessman, who'd set his sights on her for reasons she was still trying to understand after weeks of flirtatious phone calls and deep conversations about life and love and family and all the things that mattered most to her.

For the first few weeks after they met the weekend of his

daughter Cameron's wedding to Will Abbott, one of Mary's employers, she'd waited for Patrick to lose interest. Of course he would. He was *Patrick Murphy*, and she was... Well, she was just boring Mary Larkin from Vermont with a rather spectacularly uninteresting life that suited her just fine.

What in the world could they possibly have in common?

But he kept calling and he kept flirting and he kept talking about their "friendship" as if it were some sort of relationship, and honestly, how was that even possible when he lived in New York City—a place she'd never even been— and she lived in the boonies of Vermont?

It boggled her mind. This entire situation was so far outside her area of experience and understanding. She had no idea what to think or expect as this weekend together he'd talked her into was now upon them.

Would he want to... *Ugh*, she was on the verge of a full-on panic attack if she didn't get herself under control. He would meet her in Burlington, and from there, she had no idea what he had planned. He hadn't said, and she hadn't asked. It was all she could do to agree to spend a weekend with him in the first place. And he'd talked her into taking Friday off so they would have more time together.

They were going to the other side of the state, because neither of them wanted to go public yet in Butler with their friendship or relationship or whatever it was. It was madness. That's what it was. What was she doing in the back of a sleek Mercedes-Benz being driven across the state of Vermont? She'd never been driven anywhere except by friends or family members. To have someone appear at her home wearing a black suit and driving a car as nice as this one was surreal to say the least.

Everything to do with this "situation" with Patrick was surreal. He was surreal. They were about to spend two and a half days and two nights together. Surely in that time, the other shoe would drop, and she'd see the side of him he'd kept hidden from her up to now. She'd been preparing herself for how she would handle the inevitable end of this flirtation or whatever you wanted to call it.

Because it would end when he met someone else, probably a sophisticated woman who lived near him in the city. A woman like that would be far more convenient for him than she'd ever be.

As he waited for her in Burlington, she wondered if he was anywhere near as nervous as she was. When she'd talked to him earlier, he'd been without—or so it seemed to her—a care in the world. What did he have to be nervous about? He probably did stuff like this all the time. Weekends away with the flavor of the month were certainly part of his regular routine.

It wasn't like she'd never been with a guy or had a relationship. Of course she had. Back in college, she'd dated a man for three years, expecting to marry him, but he'd had other plans that didn't include her. It had taken a while to get over that heartbreak, and by the time she did, her twenties had given way to her thirties, and the pickings had gotten a lot slimmer. As her thirties led into the early forties, dating had become less of a priority than her friends, family, work and a variety of other interests that kept her busy. She was active in her church and worked at the soup kitchen that served the needy in a nearby town.

It'd been years since she'd seriously dated, and she'd never dated *anyone* like Patrick Murphy. For one thing, he was incredibly handsome—like movie star gorgeous. The one day she'd spent in his presence, at his daughter's wedding, she hadn't been able to stop staring at him like a girl with a crush rather than a mature woman with a working brain. The day he'd first come into the office with Cameron, she'd nearly tripped over her own tongue when she said hello to him.

She'd certainly heard of him, been aware of him, read about his financial exploits and real estate deals in New York, not to mention his worldwide hotel chain, especially after Cameron had come into their lives and sparked Mary's curiosity about her new friend and colleague. But something about seeing him in person was altogether different from reading about him.

He exuded charisma, charm and an easy affability that she found enormously appealing. It was almost impossible *not* to like him, and she'd tried. Oh how she'd tried to convince herself there was absolutely no point to getting involved with someone like him.

As often as she'd told herself that, however, he'd told her the opposite, that there was every good reason to get involved with him. And over time, he'd worn her down. She was no match for his relentless charm and humor and sexiness. Dear God, the man was *sexy*! Men in their fifties were supposed to be going soft in the middle and sagging at the jaw, but there was no sign of anything as human as aging—or sagging—in Patrick Murphy. No, his jaw was chiseled, and if the muscles she'd felt under his clothes while they danced at Cameron's wedding were any indication, he was a long way from a potbelly.

And he paid attention to everything she said and did. Every minute she'd spent with him, in person and on the phone, she'd never felt so "seen" or "heard" by another human being. If he was faking his interest in her, he was one hell of a gifted actor.

"We'll be arriving at our destination in about fifteen minutes, ma'am," the driver said, breaking a long silence.

Mary immediately panicked. That was nowhere near

enough time to prepare to see him again. "Thank you," she said to the driver as she dove into her purse, looking for her brush, lipstick and mirror. Oh, who was she kidding? If she had fifteen more *hours* to prepare, she still wouldn't be ready for him.

She'd dressed carefully and casually in jeans and a chocolate-brown sweater she'd bought at the Green Mountain Country Store where she worked. One of the sales associates had told her it complemented her coloring. Before she left her house, she'd scrutinized the unremarkable brown hair that she'd decided to grow out after the summer and her equally unremarkable brown eyes that had been filled with trepidation.

What the hell was I thinking agreeing to this weekend with him?

He'd wanted her to come to New York, but she was in no way ready for that, so they'd compromised, agreeing to meet in Burlington. Until this morning, she'd thought he'd agreed to her plan to drive herself. That was before the car and driver showed up at her front door, changing her plans.

"Mr. Murphy sent me to pick you up," Bob the driver had said.

"Did he now?"

Mary knew she shouldn't be surprised. Patrick had already shown her his propensity for the grand gesture in the form of the huge and breathtaking floral arrangement that had arrived at her door three days after Cameron's wedding. The card had said, "Thinking of you. P" By then, she'd assumed she wouldn't hear from him again, but the flowers had been the opening salvo in what became daily phone calls and other thoughtful gifts that showed up regularly.

As she toyed with the gorgeous silver bangle he'd sent, she recalled receiving it and having to acknowledge that he was wooing her—and she was letting him. How else to explain the insanity that had overtaken her normally rational and sane mind? How else to explain the daydreaming at work, the sleepy mornings after late-night phone calls and the powerful sense of anticipation that overtook her as they rolled into Burlington?

If he was playing her…

No. She couldn't go there. She just couldn't entertain that possibility even if it was a reasonable worry when you considered who he was and who she… *wasn't*.

They took a series of turns, and Mary was surprised when they drove through a residential area when she'd expected to end up in a hotel downtown where she'd spend the remainder of the day stressing about the sleeping arrangements. Surely he expected sex on a weekend away with a woman. That was how things worked in his world. Wasn't it?

Well, they weren't in *his* world. They were still in *hers*, and there wouldn't be sex unless she wanted it, no matter how charming or persuasive he might be.

All her determination and resolve disappeared like fine mist, however, when the car pulled into the driveway of a private home, and Patrick came out of the house to greet her. He wore faded jeans, a nondescript sweater and hiking boots. He looked rugged and sexy and every bit as gorgeous as she recalled—and nothing at all like a billionaire.

She'd been certain that her memories of the short time they'd spent together in person had to be figments of her overly active imagination. No man could ever truly be as magnetic and sexy as Patrick Murphy, or so she'd told herself.

As he opened the car door and smiled down at her, Mary realized she'd been wrong—very, *very* wrong. He was all that and so much more.

He offered a hand to help her out of the car. "I thought you'd never get here."

Her legs were stiff from the long ride. That was why they didn't want to work the way they usually did. What else could it be?

Then he leaned in and kissed her cheek, the scent of his expensive cologne filling her senses. "It's so good to see you."

She knew she should say something in response to that, but her brain had chosen this all-important moment to go entirely blank.

He took her bag from the driver and shook the man's hand. "Pick up at three on Sunday, Bob?"

"I'll be here. You have a nice weekend, Mr. Murphy, ma'am."

"Thank you. You, too." Carrying her bag, Patrick put his arm around Mary to lead her inside.

"Whose house is this?"

"Linc's."

Mary stopped walking and looked up at him in horror. "As in *Lincoln Abbott, my boss?*"

"You know another Linc? He may be your boss, but he's been my friend for more than thirty years. He's offered this place to me many times before. He was thrilled when I finally took him up on the invite."

"I can't stay here! I *work* for them. It wouldn't be right."

"You're here as *my* guest, and *I'm* his guest. It's all good."

"It's not all good, as you say. It's… unseemly."

Patrick's brows rose toward his hairline. "Are you planning to behave in an unseemly fashion?" he asked with amusement dancing in his beautiful eyes, which were hazel in some cases and blue in others, depending on the light and what color he wore.

"Of course not." Mary was quite certain her face had

7

turned an unappealing shade of tomato red. "I can't be…
here… with you."

"Are you or are you not friends with the Abbott family
after working for them for decades?"

"They are my friends, of course they are, but—"

"No buts. Look at this beautiful house with the gorgeous
view of the lake. What could be a better setting than this for
relaxing and getting to know each other better?"

The house was beautiful, that much was for certain. She
walked over to the windows for a closer look at the lake.

"You've never been here?"

"No, but I've certainly heard about it. I was sick for
Hannah's wedding, so I couldn't come."

"I wondered why I didn't meet you then."

"I had an awful sinus infection that turned into bronchitis
the week of the wedding. I was so sad to miss it."

His hands landed on her shoulders and his chin on the
top of her head, which served as a reminder of how much
taller he was—as if she needed a reminder. "If I had met you
then, I would've remembered you."

"Were you at Hannah's first wedding? I don't remember
you there."

"No, I was in China and missed it."

Surrounded by the rich citrus of his cologne, Mary
focused on breathing through the nerves that refused to let
up, especially now that she knew where they were spending
the weekend. And then another far more worrisome thought
occurred to her. "Did you tell Linc who you were meeting
here?"

"Of course I didn't. What would be the point of that? We
said we weren't ready to go public, and telling Linc would
count as going public."

"Yes, it really would. He's a terrible gossip."

Patrick massaged the tension from her shoulders. "I want you to do something for me."

"What's that?"

"I've been so looking forward to spending this time with you. I want you to relax and enjoy this weekend and not worry about anything. Can you do that?"

Taken in by the sweet words, handsome face and the sexy sound of his voice, Mary said, "I can certainly try."

CHAPTER 2

"Only I can change my life. No one else can do it for me."
—Carol Burnett

"I was thinking we could go for a hike and then maybe into town for lunch," he said. "What do you think?"

"That sounds good to me." Mary was relieved that they weren't going to hunker down in the house for the entire time they were together. It was easier to deal with her nerves and the excess emotions storming around inside her if they were out and about rather than alone together in a house full of beds.

"Linc told me about some great trails nearby that we can check out." Patrick held the door for her as they left the house and walked down the dirt road toward one of the trails. He took a deep breath of the cool fresh air. "It smells so good here, like pine and wood smoke and clean air."

"After the first time he was there, Will said he couldn't believe the wide array of bad smells he encountered in the city."

"New York is nothing if not stinky."

"Even your part of New York?"

He laughed at the teasing tone of her question. "My neighborhood isn't quite as fragrant as some of the others."

"Why am I not surprised?"

Grinning, he looked over at her.

Oh that boyish grin did weird things to her insides, just like it had the day of the wedding, the last time she'd seen him in person.

"I like the way you poke fun at me."

"I don't mean to be unkind."

"You're never unkind. You're truthful and real, and you make me see things from a whole new perspective. I like your perspective." He casually draped an arm around her shoulders, like it was no big deal when it was a huge big deal to be touched by him, to be close to him like this, even if they were strolling along a dirt path in the woods.

Everything he said and did meant something to her, more than it probably should.

"Are you really as nervous to be alone with me as you seem?" he asked.

"I wish I wasn't, but I can't help it. I have no idea what I'm doing here."

He stopped walking, dropped his arm from her shoulders and turned to face her, seeming stunned. "You really don't?"

Mary immediately missed the weight of his arm around her. "I do, but…" She rolled her bottom lip between her teeth and diverted her eyes away from the intense gaze that saw her a little too well.

Patrick framed her face in his big hands, unnerving her even further, if that was possible. "You have nothing at all to be afraid of where I'm concerned. I couldn't wait to see you again. I can't recall the last time I was this excited for a weekend."

"Me either."

Keeping his gaze fixed on hers, he lowered his head and very gently touched his lips to hers. "I couldn't wait another second to taste you."

Mary leaned into him, hoping he'd do it again.

He didn't disappoint. His lips brushed against hers in a light, undemanding caress that had her holding back a moan and a plea for more.

Just like he had the first time they spent time together, he scrambled her brain with the way he looked at her and touched her, and then he made it even worse by kissing her and setting off a firestorm inside her.

"Tell me what you're afraid of."

"I can't."

"Yes, you can. We've talked about so many things. Don't stop talking to me now when it matters so much."

"Does it?"

"Hell yes, it matters. I'm completely gone over you. You have no idea."

She drew in an unsteady breath. "Are you really?"

"Mary… God, *yes*. I think about you all the time. I count the hours until I can talk to you every day, and decline invitations and meetings that would require me to miss our nightly phone calls. My entire life is governed by the hour I get to spend with you every day. So please, sweetheart. Tell me what you're worried about so we can make it go away."

He stripped her defenses the way no other man ever had. That was why she didn't hesitate to share her deepest concern with him. "I'm afraid you're going to hurt me."

"No," he said fiercely as he wrapped his arms around her and brought her in tight against him. "Never. For the first time since I lost my wife thirty years ago, I have real, genuine, *significant* feelings for a woman. The last thing in this world I would ever do is hurt you, Mary. You have to believe me."

He had *significant* feelings for her. Oh my God. "I want to. I want to so badly."

"You can. I swear to you, if you go all in with me, you won't be sorry."

"How can I go all in with you when we live six hours from each other?"

"Logistics can be managed. Don't make that a reason to hold me at arm's length."

"I don't seem to be holding you at arm's length at the moment."

His low chuckle made her smile as she breathed in the rich, appealing scent of him.

"You smell so good," she whispered.

"Do I?"

"Mmm. Whatever it is, don't ever change it."

"If you like it, it's here to stay."

"I like it."

"I like *you*, Sweet Mary from Vermont. I'm so happy to have this time to spend with you."

With his arms around her and the scent she loved so much filling her senses, she took comfort in his assurances that she was safe with him. Mary finally relaxed, and her nerves gave way to excitement and anticipation.

LATER THAT NIGHT, THEY SAT IN FRONT OF THE FIRE PLAYING A competitive game of checkers that she was winning, but not by much.

"Are you sure you're not cheating?" he asked as he refilled both their glasses with Chardonnay. The firelight cast her in a warm glow that only made her more attractive to him. Her cheeks bore the slightest flush from the heat of the fire and the wine. Patrick remembered that wine had made her cheeks rosy at Will and Cameron's wedding. He remembered every minute he'd spent with her, and that alone made her different from any other woman he'd spent time with since he'd lost his wife.

"I do *not* cheat," she said indignantly—and adorably. "You're just mad because you win at every game you play, which makes you a sore loser when things don't go your way."

"That's very true," he replied bluntly, making her laugh. "I don't like to lose."

"I would imagine you have very little experience with losing."

"I have some." His brows furrowed as he examined the board, delight unfurling inside him when he saw the chance to win—and win big. "And I'm very sorry to say that I'm not going to add to my loser résumé tonight." With his one king, he performed a triple jump that basically wiped out her remaining checkers.

Stunned, she stared at the board where she'd been thoroughly decimated. "You did *not* just do that."

"I'm afraid it had to be done."

"That was not nice."

"No, it wasn't. But all's fair in love and checkers."

"Of course I knew you had this ruthless side to you. You don't get to where you are without being ruthless, but that… That was just…"

"Brilliant?" He loved to goad her and to watch her expressive face as she formulated what was certain to be a witty reply.

"*Evil* is the word I would use."

"I'm very sorry."

"No, you're not! And PS, I quit."

He raised an eyebrow. "You want to play Monopoly instead?"

"Absolutely not. I can't even imagine how good at that you must be."

He flashed a smug grin. "I've never lost a game of Monopoly."

"Which of course you weren't going to tell me until you thoroughly trounced me."

Her indignant comment turned him on. Hell, everything about her turned him on. If she had any idea how badly he wanted her, she'd run screaming from the house and be back in Butler before midnight. "The first key to running a successful business is to never tip your hand to the opponent."

"Oh, so now I'm your opponent. I see how it is."

Patrick laughed at her sauciness. He loved how real she always was with him when other women tended to fawn over him, plying him with insincerity to keep him interested. Mary wouldn't know how to be insincere if she tried, and as a result, she had him fiercely interested. "I'm very sorry for thoroughly trouncing you in checkers. Will you please accept my apology?"

"I will not, because I don't believe for one second that you're truly sorry."

And she was fun. So freaking *fun* to be with. They'd had the best day hiking in the woods, walking around downtown Burlington, having lunch at one of the cozy restaurants and going to a movie. Since neither of them was starving after a big lunch, they made sandwiches for dinner from the groceries he'd bought before she arrived and had decided to check out the Abbotts' game closet.

He couldn't have dreamed up a better day than the one

they'd had today. The best part was they got to do it all again tomorrow and most of Sunday, too. Patrick couldn't recall the last time he'd taken three full days away from work, but he'd left his laptop on the plane and had given his assistant very strict instructions to call him only in the event of a true emergency.

"Patrick Murphy unplugged," his assistant, Maggie, had said when he told her he'd be off the grid this weekend. "It must be love."

Her teasing comment had sent him reeling. Was he in love with Mary? The more time he spent with her, the more he suspected he might be well on his way. But he had to tread carefully with her. She was skittish and uncertain and felt out of her league with him for some reason that baffled him. *He* wasn't good enough for her, not the other way around.

"Why have you suddenly gone quiet on me?" she asked as she put away the game. "Are you trying to think of some other game you can crush me in?"

"Actually, I'm wondering if you're going to let me kiss you again."

Because he was watching her so closely, he noticed her entire body go rigid with tension that made him realize she was still uncertain where he was concerned. *We can't have that*, he thought, as he let a strand of her soft hair sift through his fingers.

"Now *you've* gone quiet on me," he said.

"I'm sorry. I don't mean to act like a middle school girl around you."

Patrick laughed. "You do not act like a middle school girl."

"Well, I feel like I'm in ninth grade and have somehow managed to attract the captain of the football team, and he's looking at me like he wants to do wicked things to me under the bleachers after the game."

The visual she created made him hard for her. "What a

vivid imagination you have." He ran his finger over the sweet blush on her cheek. "For me, it's like the sweetest girl in school has somehow agreed to spend time with me, and I'll do anything to make sure I don't screw it up with her before I ever get a chance to show her how special she is to me."

"Your imagination is rather vivid, too."

"You're not the only one who feels out of your league here, Mary."

"How is that possible? You're Patrick Murphy, for crying out loud."

"Forget all the hype and the BS that goes with being Patrick Murphy. Right here and now, I'm just a guy who desperately wants to kiss his girl."

Her gaze flickered to his lips as she licked her own.

I'm a fucking goner for her, Patrick thought. Watching the subtle movement of her tongue over her lip had him clinging to the edge of reason.

"Desperately, huh?"

"Incredibly desperately." Was it wishful thinking on his part or did she lean in a little closer to him? No, definitely not wishful thinking… He put his arm around her. "Come here, sweetheart."

She hesitated, but only for a moment before she moved closer to him.

It had been a very long time—decades, in fact—since Patrick had felt as uncertain around a woman as he did with her. It had been just as long since he'd wanted a woman the way he wanted her—in every way it was possible to have her. "Tell me this is what you want. That I'm what you want."

"I'd have to be dead to not want you, Patrick." After a short pause, she said, "I'm sorry. I shouldn't have said it that way. I don't mean to be insensitive."

"It's okay. I liked the sentiment behind it." Smiling, he leaned in and forced himself to go slow, to be gentle and tender rather than ravenous, which was how she made him feel, as if he were starving for her. The instant his lips connected with hers, he understood two things very clearly. One, he was absolutely in love with her, and two, moving slowly for her was going to be one of the biggest challenges he'd faced in his entire life.

CHAPTER 3

*"We must let go of the life we had planned,
so as to accept the one that is waiting for us."*
—Joseph Campbell

he man knows how to kiss. Sweet Jesus, could he kiss. His lips were soft and persuasive and… Oh God, he was using his tongue to convince her to open her mouth and allow him in. She didn't need much convincing after the amazing day she'd spent with him. It felt so damned good to be held and kissed by him, to be close to him this way after a month of buildup that she now knew had been leading to *this*.

Desire could be a fickle thing. One handsome man could do nothing for you, while another could set your entire body on fire with desire the way Patrick was currently doing to her. He had one hand cradling her face and the other buried in her hair to anchor her to him while he kissed her senseless. She must've taken leave of her senses. How else to explain that her tongue was currently flirting with his while the rest of her wished it could get in on the fun her mouth was having?

Patrick seemed to be thinking the same thing, because, without breaking the kiss, he moved them so they were stretched out on the floor in front of the fire, his leg between hers and their bodies tightly aligned. He tasted like wine and sexy man, and he was making her crave things she'd never craved before.

Mary had enjoyed sex with previous lovers, but it hadn't been anything like this, and all they'd done so far was kiss. But to call *this* a "kiss" would be vastly understating the power of what it was doing to her. With every stroke of his tongue, he shredded what remained of her defenses, leaving her feeling raw and exposed to whatever might happen next.

He'd told her it was okay to feel safe with him and that he'd take care not to hurt her. She could only hope he'd be true to his word, because there would be no turning back after this weekend.

He finally broke the kiss, and they both took deep breaths as he turned his attention to her neck. "God, you're so sweet. I love kissing you." His hand snuck under the back of her sweater, branding her skin with his heat and making her tremble from the power of the desire he stirred in her.

"Tell me to stop and I will," he whispered against her ear in the second before he bit down gently but insistently on her earlobe.

"Don't stop," Mary said, surprising herself and him, too, judging by the way he looked at her. "Not yet."

After gazing down at her for an intense moment, he kissed her again, this time going straight for the good stuff, tongue twisting with tongue as his hand moved from the back of her sweater to the front and up to cup her breast through the sexy bra she'd bought with him in mind. Just in case things progressed on this weekend together... She'd wanted to be prepared, but nothing could've prepared her for *this* or how it would feel to be consumed by him.

He rubbed his thumb back and forth over her rigid nipple.

Mary gasped and broke the kiss, needing her wits about her to contend with the sensations spiraling from where he touched her, all of them converging in a throb between her legs.

"Talk to me, sweetheart," he whispered gruffly. "Tell me what you want."

"I... I'm not sure what I want."

"If it's too much too soon, all you have to do is say so." As he spoke, he continued the gentle sweep of his thumb over her nipple. "You won't hurt my feelings."

"It doesn't feel like too much or too soon." She reached up to caress the face of the man who had—one phone call and email and thoughtful gift at a time—become the center of her world over the last month.

"I'm glad to hear you say that, because I've been going crazy wanting to see you again. If you hadn't agreed to this weekend, I might've had to show up on your doorstep and hope you wouldn't turn me away."

"I wouldn't have turned you away. I wanted to see you just as badly."

He nuzzled her neck, and she broke out in goose bumps. "I want to kiss you here," he said, tweaking her nipple between his fingers. "I want to kiss you everywhere." Patrick dragged his fingertips down her belly to tug on the button to her jeans, letting her know what he meant by everywhere.

Mary trembled wildly under his touch. He had aroused her to the point of madness, and all he'd done was kiss and touch her. Here she stood on the precipice of fully diving into this thing with him and letting the chips fall where they may. In the midst of this sensually charged interlude, she couldn't spare the brain cells to care about where the chips might fall. She just wanted him.

"I want you to," she said haltingly.

"What do you want me to do?" His lips skimmed her neck. "Tell me."

"I… I want you to kiss me. Everywhere."

His low groan let her know what he thought of her request. "Here or in bed?"

Mary was afraid that if they took the time to relocate, she might lose her nerve. "Here. For now."

He tugged on her sweater. "Can we take this off?"

"Only if we take yours off, too."

"We can do that." He helped her out of hers and then removed his.

Mary drank in her first look at the muscular, well-honed chest that he'd been hiding under his clothes and licked her lips. "I knew it," she said.

"What did you know?" he asked, his eyes warm with amusement.

"That you were all muscle under there."

"I have a trainer who works me like the spawn of Satan that he is. He refuses to let me get flabby in my old age."

She flattened her hand on his pectoral and dragged it down to cover the six-pack on his abdomen. "I would like for you to double his salary."

"Done. I'll tell him on Monday. He'll be thrilled."

"Stop. I was kidding."

"I'm not. If the fruits of his labors are you looking at me like that, he deserves twice what I'm paying him."

Mary smiled at him. "You're crazy."

"Maybe so, but that would be money very well spent." He kissed his way from her neck to her collarbone and then down to the plump tops of her breasts. "But I don't want to talk about him when I'd much rather talk about you and how stunningly beautiful you are."

No man had ever said such things to her before. She took a shuddering deep breath and raised her hands to comb her fingers through his thick hair that had once been blond but was now more gray than blond. On him, the gray only added to his sexiness. It was easy to forget who he was and what he had when they were close to each other this way, but always in the back of her mind was the nagging doubt about how a man like him could ever be interested in her long-term.

"Why did you just get all tense on me?" he asked.

"Did I?"

"Uh-huh. What're you thinking about?"

"Whether I can hold your attention long-term." The words were out before she took the time to decide whether she should say them.

He raised his head to meet her gaze, seeming shocked. "Why would you wonder that? If you only knew how interested in you I am."

Mary instantly regretted interrupting what they'd been doing to air her insecurities. "I believe you when you say that, but… Never mind. It doesn't matter."

"It does matter. It matters greatly to me that you think you aren't enough for me."

"You live a big exciting life. Mine is small and simple and actually kind of boring. I don't want you to be bored by me."

"Mary… God, did I seem bored for one second today? I can't get enough of you. Everything you say interests me. My life might look big and exciting from the outside looking in, but in reality, it's actually very lonely most of the time."

"How can that be when you're surrounded by people?"

"Have you ever been in a crowd and felt alone?"

"I can't say that I have."

"Then you haven't really experienced what it's like to be

lost in a crowd with no one you care about anywhere in sight. Being surrounded by people all the time isn't as satisfying as you might think."

It pained her to hear that his life was so lonely.

"I don't want you to ever think you're not enough for me. I've been a whole lot less lonely since I met you and get to look forward to talking to you every day."

"I'm glad to hear that. I feel the same way. My life was always very satisfying to me, but now it's more so."

"It makes me happy to know that I've done that for you, because you've given me so much. More than you can possibly know."

"I'm sorry if I got insecure and ruined the mood."

He pressed his erection against her leg. "My mood isn't ruined. Is yours?"

She laughed at the adorably boyish expression on his face and reached up to place her hand on his face to bring him down for another of those amazing kisses. Who could be bothered with insecurities when a hot, sexy, *nice* man wanted her as badly as he seemed to?

PATRICK FELT HER GIVE IN TO HIM, HER WALLS DROPPING LIKE dominoes to allow him in. She kissed him with wild abandon that had him fighting for control of a situation that was rapidly spinning out of control.

His plan to take it slow was being obliterated by her enthusiastic kisses and sexy moans. Reaching behind her, he released the hooks on her bra and eased the straps down her arms, holding his breath as he revealed her breasts. Christ, she was lovely. Her breasts were small but sensitive, judging from the way she'd reacted to him touching her earlier.

Leaning over her, he drew her nipple into his mouth,

sucking lightly as he pinched the other one between his fingers.

Gasping, she fisted a handful of his hair, and when he ran his tongue over the tight pink tip, she arched into him, the heat of her core against his cock making him crave more of her.

"Mary…" He dropped his forehead to her chest. "Tell me to stop."

"Do you want to stop?"

Raising his head so he could see her face, he said, "God, no, but I don't want you to think this is the only reason I wanted to spend the weekend with you."

"So you weren't hoping for this?" she asked with a teasing smile.

"Umm, how to answer that in the most diplomatic way possible…"

"Just tell me the truth."

"I've hoped I'd get a chance to hold you and kiss you and make love with you." He nuzzled her breast. "Since the day I met you." Glancing at her face again, he added, "But I don't want to rush you or push you for things you're not ready for."

Mary crooked her finger at him. "Come here."

Patrick came down on top of her.

She ran her fingers through his hair. "I was nervous about whether this would happen."

"And now?"

"Now," she said, driving him crazy with the scratch of her nails over his scalp. He hadn't known his scalp was an erogenous zone until she showed him. "I don't feel nervous anymore," she said. "I feel…"

Patrick held his breath, waiting to hear what she'd say. "What do you feel, honey?"

"Needy."

He released a long exhale. "I'll give you whatever you need, Sweet Mary. Anything at all."

"I just need you."

"You have me." He brushed the hair back from her face. "I'm right here, and I'm all yours."

"For how long?" she asked, looking madly vulnerable.

His heart beat double time. "For as long as you want me."

"That could be a while."

"I'm cool with that."

Her smile lit up his world. He had to kiss her or die from wanting to. Tilting his head, he brought his lips down on hers and lost himself in her. He hadn't felt anything like this since Ali died thirty years ago, and after waiting all that time to find Mary, he would never let her go.

MARY HADN'T EXPECTED TO GET SO CAUGHT UP IN HIM THAT she'd be hoping he would suggest they sleep together. So much for playing it cool and taking it slow. He'd completely disarmed her with passionate kisses and the reverent way he touched her. She lacked the vocabulary to ask him for what she wanted, which made her feel stupid and frustrated.

His finger traced the furrow between her brows. "What's this about?"

"I... I don't know how to tell you..."

With his fingers on her chin, he forced her to meet his gaze. "Mary, honey, whatever it is you want to say, just say it. Whatever it is, I promise you I want to hear it. I wish I could know everything about you."

His open honesty made it easier for her to level with him.

"I want to go to bed. With you. Now."

"Are you sleepy?"

She shook her head. "I'm wide awake."

"Is that right?"

"Uh-huh."

His smile unfolded slowly across his sinfully handsome face. "Why Sweet Mary from Vermont, are you propositioning me?"

"What if I am?"

"I'd be the happiest guy in the entire world." He raised himself up and offered her a hand.

She felt self-conscious about strutting around half-naked in front of him, even if she had just propositioned him.

Of course, he knew that and wrapped a soft throw around her shoulders.

"Thank you."

"Sure," he said, gathering her hair and lifting it free of the blanket.

"I can't believe I'm rolling around on the floor of Linc and Molly's house and wrapped up in their blanket and about to sleep with you in one of their beds."

"Are we just going to sleep? Because that'd be kinda disappointing after the proposition."

She laughed as she groaned. "Stop tormenting me."

"Why would I do that when it's so much fun to torment you?" He led her into the first-floor master suite, where his duffel bag sat at the foot of the bed. "Let me go grab your bag real quick."

Mary sat on the bed and drew the blanket in tighter around her, feeling the burst of courage disappear now that she was in the room where Lincoln and Molly slept at the house. It felt weird to think about having sex with Patrick in their bed.

Patrick returned with her suitcase, which he left next to the door and came over to sit next to her. "Are you cold?"

"What? No. Why?"

"You're holding on to that blanket for dear life."

"Oh. Well…"

27

"It's okay, Mary. Everything is okay." He put his arm around her and kissed her temple. "I'm so happy to be here with you, no matter what happens or what doesn't."

"I'm the worst kind of tease."

"No, you're not. You're a refreshing change of pace."

She glanced at him. "What does that mean?"

"I've always heard it's a bad idea to talk about other women with the woman you are currently hoping to spend more time with."

Mary scowled at him. "Tell me what you meant."

Patrick sighed and looked down. "It has been my experience that most women are interested in two things when they get involved with me—what I can buy them and what I can do for them. It's rarely ever about me. With you, for the first time since I lost my wife, I feel like you're here because of me, not because of the money or the notoriety or the other BS that goes along with being me."

"Patrick," she said on a long exhale, slightly appalled to hear how shamelessly women had used him. "You have to know by now that I don't care about any of that stuff."

He looked at her and rested a finger on her lips. "I know, sweetheart. That's what I meant when I said you were refreshing. Everything about this has been refreshing and exciting and a little nerve-racking from the beginning."

"Why has it been nerve-racking? I mean, I know why it's been for me, but I'm surprised to hear you say it's been that way for you, too. You're always so confident about everything."

"Not everything," he said with a laugh. "You, my sweet, sweet Mary, have led me on a merry chase."

"I have not. Don't say that."

"Yes, you have, and that's not a bad thing. You've made me work for it, and that makes everything about this…" He leaned in to kiss her. "So much more satisfying."

"I'm glad you feel that way. I don't mean to play hard to get."

"You're not. You're being cautious, and I respect that. Let's get ready for bed—and if you don't want to sleep in here with me, that's totally fine."

"Could we, maybe, sleep in one of the other bedrooms? This one has to be Linc and Molly's, and it's just weird for me to be sleeping in my boss's bed."

Smiling, he said, "Of course we can relocate."

"It's okay. You can go ahead and make fun of me. I know I'm full of weird hang-ups."

"You're perfect just the way you are. Go on upstairs and pick any room you want, and I'll bring our stuff up."

"Okay." Holding the blanket tight around her, she went up the stairs thinking about how sweet he was, how accommodating and understanding. His easygoing attitude toward just about everything made it easy to forget that he was one of the wealthiest men in the world.

Mary poked her head into a couple of bedrooms before choosing one that would have a daytime view of the lake. It also had an adjoining bathroom and, more importantly, a king-sized bed.

"Find something?" he asked when he appeared in the doorway with their bags.

"This will work."

"You want to use the bathroom first?"

"Sure." She took the handle of her small weekender bag and wheeled it into the bathroom where she changed into flannel pajamas with snowflakes on them, because nothing said sexy like flannel and snowflakes, brushed her hair and teeth and tried to get her nerves back under control. It had been a long, long time since she'd shared a bed with a man, and she'd never shared a bed with a man who wanted her the way Patrick did—and vice versa. She'd heard about the kind of heated attraction that flared between them and had seen it between couples she knew, including his daughter and her husband, but she'd never experienced it herself, not like this anyway.

Staring at her reflection in the mirror, she took a series of deep, calming breaths, calling herself every kind of fool for being so nervous around him when he'd gone out of his way to put her at ease. "Relax and stop being such a nitwit."

She threw open the door to find Patrick sitting on the bed wearing red plaid flannel pajama pants and scrolling through his phone. Dark-framed glasses made him sexier than he already was, if that was possible.

He looked up at her as he stashed the phone on the bedside table. "You say something, hon?"

"No," she said, embarrassed that he'd overheard her pep talk. "Bathroom is all yours."

"I'll be quick," he said, kissing her cheek on the way by.

Mary got into bed, wondering if he preferred one side or the other. She usually slept on the right side at home, so that was where she settled in, tugging the covers up to her chin. The bed was warm and soft, and she recognized the navy-and-green-plaid flannel duvet cover from the store.

Patrick came out of the bathroom a few minutes later, and Mary's gaze went directly to his chest, which was still bare. He took off his glasses and left them on the bedside table, where he plugged in his phone before getting into bed.

"Are you okay on that side?" she asked.

"This is fine, but you are way too far away over there." He held out his arm to her. "Come here."

Mary scooted over and snuggled up to him, her face on his chest, her hand on his stomach, which quivered under the heat of her palm.

He tightened his arm around her and nuzzled her hair.

"That's much better. And by the way, you're very cute in those jammies."

"You're pretty cute in your jammies, too, but you forgot your shirt."

"I didn't forget. I rarely wear anything to bed."

Mary felt her face get very warm when she realized he'd worn the pajama pants for her. The thought of him sleeping nude made her feel warm all over.

"Sorry I was checking my phone before. I was waiting for an email from Cam about her and Will coming down to the city for a visit after I get back from China and Japan. I miss being able to text her now that she lives in the cell phone never-never land known as Butler."

"You're going to China and Japan?" Mary hadn't heard much of what he said after the word "China."

"I'm leaving for two weeks on Tuesday. I told you that."

"I don't think you did," she said, feeling oddly deflated to know he'd be so far away for such a long time. What did it matter, she asked herself, when he already lived six hours from her?

He looked down at her. "You want to come with me?"

CHAPTER 4

"Life isn't about finding yourself.
Life is about creating yourself."
—George Bernard Shaw

ary groaned, filled with regret and frustration that she couldn't take him up on the offer. She didn't have a spur-of-the-moment bone in her body, for one thing. "I don't have a passport, which makes me sound like a small-town hick next to your world-traveling self."

"Not at all. We could get you one if you want to come. I have contacts at the State Department who'd help me out. I'd love to have you. Just say the word."

"I can't pick up and go away for two weeks. I have a job and a life and…" Really, she had no good reason at all to say no to the trip of a lifetime.

"I understand."

"I'm glad you do, because I'm furious that I can't go. I've never been anywhere, and I want to go everywhere."

"Come with me, Mary. I'll take you around the world. We'll go anywhere you want."

"You're like the devil himself, Patrick. Temptation personified."

"Why thank you, honey. That might be the nicest compliment anyone has ever paid me."

She snorted with laughter. "You would take someone calling you a tempting devil as a compliment."

"Not just anyone. I like it when *you* say it."

"So you'll be gone for Thanksgiving?" she asked.

"Uh-huh. I figured with Cam set with her new family this year, there was no reason to put off meetings in countries that don't celebrate the holiday. Of course, I decided that before I met you." He combed his fingers through her hair. "What're you doing for the holiday?"

"I work at the soup kitchen every year. It's one of our busiest days."

"You do so much for others. It's very admirable."

"I enjoy it." She propped her head on his chest. "Could I ask you something?"

"Anything you want."

"You mentioned your wife a couple of times. Would you tell me about her?" Only because she was lying so close to him did she feel the tension that came over him and immediately regretted ruining their playful mood by bringing up a difficult subject for him. "You don't have to if you don't want to. I didn't mean to spoil our good time. It's none of my business."

He rested a finger over her lips. "It's not that I don't want to. It's just… It's still hard to talk about even almost thirty years later."

"I'm sorry, Patrick. I didn't mean to open an old wound."

"You didn't. That wound has never really healed."

"Of course it didn't. How could it?"

"I met Ali my first week at NYU. I was there on an academic scholarship, and she worked in the cafeteria."

MARIE FORCE

"Was she a student, too?"

"No, she was helping to support her family. Her mom died having her youngest sister, the dad was emotionally unstable, and they were in dire financial straits. She worked three jobs to help keep them afloat." He got a faraway look in his eyes. "She was the most beautiful girl I'd ever seen. Cameron looks just like she did when we first met, which has been very difficult for me at times. Ali and I saw each other as much as we could between school and work. She did a lot for her younger sisters, too, so we were lucky to get two or three hours a week together, sometimes late at night or first thing in the morning. But we took what we could get. I never dated anyone else the entire time I was in college, and right before graduation, I proposed. Her dad was vehemently opposed to her getting married. I think it was because he needed her so much to help out with her siblings, but he said things… Awful things that hurt us both and put a rift between us and her family that broke her heart. I actually offered to step aside to make things easier for her, but she wouldn't hear of that."

"She loved you."

"She really did, and I loved her so much." He took a deep breath. "We were really happy together as I started my business. We lived on love and ramen noodles for a few years before things started to take off a little. We got pregnant with Cam, and she was so excited, especially after we learned we were having a little girl. She came up with the name Cameron when she was about five months along, and wouldn't consider any other name. I wanted what she wanted, so I was fine with it. Then her labor started, and it went sideways from the beginning. She was in labor for two days, and the baby wouldn't come. They talked about a C-section, but she really didn't want that, and I was stuck on the sidelines watching her suffer and feeling so helpless.

34

"Cameron finally showed up in the middle of the second night, the most perfect baby you've ever seen. And Ali... She was so tired, and she'd lost a lot of blood. They had trouble getting it to stop and were talking about doing a hysterectomy when her heart stopped."

"Oh, Patrick..." Mary wiped at tears.

"They tried to revive her. Worked on her for more than an hour. I couldn't believe it was possible to lose her that way. She was young and healthy and strong. When they came out to tell me, I already knew. I felt dead inside, even before they said the words. So, there I was with a newborn, a fledgling business that needed my full attention and my heart broken into a million pieces. I had no idea how I was supposed to go on without her. I was twenty-four years old, and I felt like my life was over."

"I'm so sorry that happened to you and to Cameron."

"I ran into one of Ali's sisters a couple of years after she died, and she told me what happened to Ali was the same thing that happened to their mother when she had their youngest sister. So now I get to live in mortal fear of that happening to my daughter when or if she decides to have children."

"Oh my God," Mary whispered. "Does she know that her grandmother also died from childbirth?"

"No. I never told her because I didn't want her to be afraid of dying young."

"You have to tell her, Patrick. She has a right to know."

"I will. They said they're not in any rush to have kids, so I figure I have some time before I bring that up with her. Not that there's any right time to tell someone you love that having babies could be a bad idea."

"Still," Mary said, wiping away new tears at the thought of something so terrible happening to Cameron, Will and Patrick. "You have to tell her."

"I will when I see her over the holidays. I've done some research, talked to a lot of doctors, and everyone tells me so much has changed in thirty years, and there's no reason to think that what happened to her mother and grandmother will definitely happen to her, too. There's also no way to know for sure that the same exact thing happened to both of them, other than they both died as the result of childbirth."

"That's somewhat reassuring."

"Is it wrong of me to hope she never decides to have kids?"

"No, of course not."

"I'm not sure how I'd survive if something ever happened to her. I wasn't always a good father to her, but God, I love her."

"I know you do, and I'm sure you were a great father to her."

"No, I really wasn't. I was gone more than I was home, and I let a progression of nannies and other people I paid do most of the heavy lifting with her. I didn't even know she has attention deficit disorder until she was in college and figured it out for herself. I spent twelve years deriding her for her lousy grades and telling her to quit being lazy about her schoolwork. It made me crazy that her grades were so bad. And you know what? She never told me about the ADD. Lucy let it slip by accident. She said something about how they'd bonded over their ADD issues."

"That must've been hard to hear."

"It was awful. I went home and looked it up, and when I read about it, I was in tears thinking about all the terrible shit I'd said to her. It never once occurred to me that anything was wrong. Her mother would've been all over that, and I... I was just clueless. I still feel bad about that all these years later and even after I apologized to her for the way I treated her."

"You did the best you could in an awful situation."

"I really didn't, Mary. I appreciate you trying to make me feel better, but I'm always going to have to live with the guilt of knowing I left my little girl to fend for herself in an unforgiving world while I was off building my empire."

"She was well cared for. I'm sure you saw to that."

"Always, but what she wanted most was me, and I didn't give her that."

"You were heartbroken and grief-stricken to have lost your wife the way you did. I'm sure that had something to do with the decisions you made during those years."

"I don't remember much about the first few years after Ali died. It's all a blur."

"You just proved my point. Cameron loves you very much. That's obvious to anyone who has seen the two of you together. You guys were so sweet at the wedding when you gave her away. You both had tears in your eyes. You made me cry."

"She wore her mom's dress and surprised me with it. I was floored by that."

"I can only imagine how emotional that must've made you."

"I was a total disaster that day. You saved me from embarrassing myself by keeping me company."

Mary smiled at him. "It was a terrible job, but someone had to do it."

His eyes lit up as he returned her smile, obliterating the grief that had overtaken him. "Thanks for listening to all that terribly sad stuff."

"Thank you for sharing it with me." She reached out to caress his face and drew him into a kiss that started off slow and sweet and quickly spiraled into something much needier and urgent. Hearing what he'd endured and how he'd admitted to his failings as a father made him that much more

37

human to her—and that much more appealing. He was living proof that no one got through life unscathed, no matter how fortunate they might appear to others.

Mary felt his hand on her pajama top, realized he was unbuttoning it, and did nothing to stop him as he spread the two panels and bared her breasts to his greedy stare. Just that quickly, he had her right back to where she'd been on the floor in front of the fire, wanting more of him and hoping he would keep going this time. If he did, she wouldn't stop him.

His hand on her breast made her gasp and then wriggle closer to him. She couldn't get close enough. On the way to Burlington, she'd thought about how no one could be as amazing as he seemed, and she'd been certain then that she'd see something in him this weekend that made him less appealing. If anything, the opposite had happened. Every bit of himself that he revealed to her, even the hard-to-hear things, made him more attractive to her, not less.

The chemistry that had been present between them since the day they met ignited once again, hotter than ever. He was changing her life one kiss at a time, one tender caress at a time, with every confidence shared, and even when he teased her or kicked her ass in checkers.

Mary was powerless to resist him, and as he kissed a path from her lips to her breasts, she felt the door to her heart open to admit him. He had worked his way under her skin so deeply that she no longer remembered what her life was like before Patrick. Now, there was only after Patrick, and after Patrick was a rather exciting place to be.

He tugged her nipple into the heat of his mouth, dragging his tongue back and forth over her sensitive flesh and setting off a firestorm that heated her entire body. In all her life, she'd never experienced the sort of craving desire that he aroused in her. The tiny part of her addled brain that continued to worry about this whole thing blowing up in her face urged caution, but her brain was quickly overruled by the rest of her that wanted anything and everything he had to give.

"God, Mary, I could do this for hours and never get enough," he whispered, his lips vibrating against her other nipple.

"Don't stop. Please don't stop." She sounded frantic and needy. In her right mind, she would've obsessed over how desperate she must've sounded to him. But in her Patrick-addled mind, she couldn't bother to care about such trivial things.

His lips moved to her belly, leaving soft, damp kisses that made her crazy for more. Then she felt his tongue dip into her belly button, and she nearly levitated right off the bed. "Easy, Mary. I'll take care of you."

Mary closed her eyes and focused on breathing, but was aware of him removing her pajama pants and panties. His fingers skimmed over her skin, which erupted in goose bumps. Then she felt his lips on her calf and the back of her knee and her inner thigh. Her body became one giant quiver with every nerve ending on alert. The surface of her skin had never been so sensitive.

Realizing his intended destination, Mary sat up, uncertain of whether she planned to push him away or pull him closer. "Patrick…"

"Shhh, let me love you." He looked up at her with fire in his eyes. "Relax, sweetheart. I'll make you feel so good."

Powerless to resist the overpowering desire he roused in her, she fell back onto the pillow as he used his broad shoulders to hold her legs wide open.

Oh my God. I'm never going to survive him. This act had never been her favorite thing, but that was probably because she'd never done it with Patrick, who clearly knew exactly what he was doing as he spread her open and gave her his tongue and fingers. He knew just where to touch her to bring her pleasure unlike anything she'd experienced before. To think she might've never known that *this* was possible had she not met him... That thought made her inordinately sad for the person she'd been before him, before this.

And then he applied the perfect amount of suction in exactly the right place as his fingers stroked her from the inside. Mary ignited, screaming his name as the orgasm powered through her, leaving her gasping in the aftermath as her body quaked with aftershocks she felt from her scalp to the soles of her feet.

"Mmm," he said, his lips vibrating against her belly while his fingers remained embedded in her. "I knew it would be amazing with you."

Mary was too busy trying to remember to breathe to formulate a coherent reply.

"Do we need protection?" he asked.

His question brought her back to reality. This was really happening, and she wanted it so badly. She wanted *him*.

"N-no. I'm safe if you are."

"I am. I had a full physical two weeks ago. I can show you—"

She reached up to place her fingers over his lips. "I trust you."

"That means everything to me."

Mary ran her hands down his back to the waistband of his pajama pants, helping him to remove them, her eyes bugging at the sight of his hard cock—his extremely large hard cock. "*Really?*" she asked. "That face, more money than God and *that*, too? You really are inordinately blessed, aren't you?"

Laughing, he said, "Not always, but lately I have been. And by the way, are you complaining?"

She eyed him with trepidation, hoping she'd be able to take him. "Could I let you know after?"

His laughter lit up his handsome face.

God, he is beautiful to look at.

Propped on his elbows above her, he brushed the hair back from her face and kissed her with lips that tasted of her.

Her heart pounded so hard, she feared it would burst through her chest.

"We'll go nice and slow," he said as he took himself in hand and ran his cock through the wetness between her legs, nudging her clit and drawing another gasp from her. "Nice and easy." He began to enter her in small increments, giving her a little before retreating and starting over.

Mary clung to his arms, feeling his biceps flex each time he pushed into her.

"Tell me how it feels," he said in a tense-sounding tone she hadn't heard from him before.

"Tight," she said. "Hot."

"Mmmm, those are good words. You feel so amazing. I want you so badly. I haven't wanted anyone the way I want you in so damned long. I'd given up on ever feeling this way again, and then there you were. My sweet, sweet Mary."

His words were as powerful as the deepening thrusts of his cock.

Mary raised her hips to meet him, drawing a groan from him as he gave her more. His chest hair brushed against her sensitive nipples, setting off a chain reaction of need that converged into a pulsating heartbeat between her legs. Sex had never, ever, *ever* been like this...

He kissed her neck, her throat and her jaw on the way to her lips. "Wrap your legs around my hips, sweetheart. Mmmm, yeah, just like that."

The new position allowed him to go deeper, and Mary started to climb toward another peak.

"So good," he whispered gruffly against her ear. "So, *so* good." He reached beneath her to grasp her bottom in his big hands, opening her even more to his deep possession.

The word "impaled" took on new meaning as he continued to give her more of himself until she wondered how much more there could possibly be. Quite a bit, as it turned out. By the time she felt his belly tight against hers, she had been stretched to her absolute limit and her inner muscles were twitching and contracting in what felt like mini-orgasms.

"Christ," he muttered. "Being inside you has to be what heaven feels like." He kissed her softly at first and then with growing urgency as he began to move in her.

Mary held on for dear life, her hands sliding down his back to grasp his muscular ass, which flexed under her hands every time he thrust into her, touching places deep inside her that she hadn't known existed until he showed her.

An orgasm took her by surprise, exploding within her like a sunburst, making her feel more in that one instant than in any other.

"Mary," he gasped, pressing deep into her to ride it out with her before giving in to his own release. He came down on top of her, and Mary wrapped her arms around him, wanting to hold on to this perfect moment—and him—for as long as she could.

His breath was warm against her neck as his heart beat hard against her chest. "Holy moly," he whispered after a long silence.

Mary laughed at the sense of wonder he conveyed in those two little words.

"Are you okay?" he asked, raising his head to look down at her.

"Mmm, much better than okay. You?"

"Same." He gazed down at her, his heart in his eyes as he

kissed her softly and sweetly even as he continued to thrust into her in gentle strokes that quickly became more as he recovered in record time and started all over again.

"I... *Patrick*... Are you out to cripple me?"

"Hardly," he said. "I just want more of you."

How could she possibly argue with that?

CHAPTER 5

"Be happy for this moment.
This moment is your life."
—Omar Khayyam

*T*hey barely left the bed on Saturday, getting up to eat and shower together before going back for more.

"I'm not going to be able to walk if we keep this up," Mary said as they watched the sunset on Saturday night. With his head on her belly, she stroked her fingers through his hair. "I've had more sex today than I've had in the last ten years combined."

"I don't want to ever think about you doing this with anyone but me."

Mary gave his hair a gentle tug. "I'm sure your recent track record is much more *checkered* than mine."

"You're still mad that I beat you in checkers, aren't you?"

"Nice attempt to change the subject."

His low chuckle made her smile. She loved making him

laugh. "How will I ever let you leave me tomorrow? You've got me completely addicted to you." He flattened his hand on her leg, slid it up the inside of her thigh and buried his fingers in her again.

She gasped and then grimaced from the pinch of pain.

"You're sore," he said, slowing the stroke of his fingers.

"Anyone would be sore after taking that beast of yours as many times as I have in the last twenty-four hours."

"On behalf of my beast, I'm wounded. We thought you liked him."

"I do like him. I like him too much."

"No such thing."

He surprised the hell out of her when he shifted to add his tongue to the party down below, bringing his cock within striking distance of her mouth.

She had never been in this position before, but she'd certainly heard about it and wondered what it might be like. She reached up to wrap her hand around his erection, stroking him the way he'd told her he liked it—a little rough and fast. "Come here," she said, licking her lips in anticipation.

He stopped what he was doing to her long enough to realize what she wanted and repositioned himself to give it to her. "Mary…"

"Hmm?" she asked, making sure her lips vibrated against his shaft.

"Christ have mercy," he said on a long gasp.

His reaction made her smile, but then she turned her focus on bringing him the kind of pleasure he'd given her. With his palms flat against her thighs, he pushed her legs farther apart and drove her wild while she tried to do the same to him. It was the most intimate thing she'd ever done, and the forbidden thrill of it only added to the excitement she felt as she took him as far into her mouth as she could get him.

His legs trembled wildly under her hands, and she could feel him trying to hold back from the need to plunge himself deeper into her mouth. All the while, he drove her mad with his fingers and tongue until he had her coming so hard, she had to release him so she wouldn't hurt him.

"Fuck," he growled. "Don't stop, Mary. God, don't stop."

His desperation fueled her as she stroked him to a quick finish. He came all over her breasts and belly. She loved the way he completely lost control and surrendered to her. It was the earthiest and most erotic thing she'd ever done. Landing on the bed next to her, he took a couple of deep breaths, his arm resting on his forehead. Then he seemed to collect himself and got up. "Let me get a towel."

He returned with a hand towel that he used to mop up the mess he'd made of her chest and abdomen. His gaze shifted to her face, and their eyes met and held, the connection between them crackling and electric. Leaning forward, he kissed her. "That," he said, "was crazy."

Mary smiled and nodded, letting her gaze travel over his naked body. Even after twenty-four hours in bed with him, she hadn't gotten tired of looking at him. Apparently, he hadn't gotten tired of looking at her either. He stared at her with a look of stunned amazement that had to match hers.

She reached for him, and he crawled into her embrace, burying his face in her hair and breathing her in. It made her feel better that he seemed equally undone by their lovemaking. For the longest time, they held each other close and breathed the same air, the aftermath as intimate as the lovemaking.

"What're we going to do about this situation?" he asked after a long, comfortable silence.

"I have no idea."

"How am I ever going to let you leave me tomorrow?"

"I don't know that either." The thought of leaving him made her feel queasy and unsettled, so she tried not to think about that. Not now, when they had all night and most of tomorrow before they had to deal with leaving each other.

"Are you sure you can't come to China with me?"

She had the vacation time, and he said he could get her a passport, and God, she *wanted* to go. But she couldn't just drop everything for two weeks with hardly any notice. She had responsibilities and obligations that couldn't be shirked because it would be fun to run away with him. "I'm sure. I can't leave work without giving Linc some notice that I'll be gone, especially this time of year when the holiday season is getting underway. He and Molly are going to England soon, so I really can't be gone at the same time he is. And I have other things, too."

"Tell me about your other things." As he spoke, he ran his fingers through her hair. "I want to know everything."

"I help out at my church and a local soup kitchen, and I'm hosting book club next week. Then there's Mildred, the oldest employee at the store. We all help with whatever she needs. I drive her to church on Sundays and bring her dinner once or twice a week."

"Who's driving her tomorrow?"

"Charley Abbott. She does Mildred's grocery shopping, so I asked if she'd mind taking her to church. Charley isn't much of a churchgoer, but she said she'd do it for Mildred." Mary glanced at him. "It all must sound so terribly boring to you."

"No, it sounds lovely, actually. You take care of each other, look out for one another. It must be nice to be part of such a community."

47

"It is. I can't imagine any other kind of life."

"Could you imagine…"

"What?"

"I thought better of what I was going to say."

"That's not fair." She poked his shoulder playfully. "Now I need to know."

"I was going to ask," he said tentatively, "if you might be able to picture yourself in a Park Avenue penthouse."

Mary's heart skipped a crazy beat as his meaning registered with her. "Ummm, since I've never been anywhere near Park Avenue, it would be very difficult to picture myself there."

"We'll have to rectify that very soon. I want you to come see my world. Do you think we might be able to make that happen?"

Mary nodded, even though she wondered if she would stick out as the small-town girl she was in his world.

"Stop frowning," he said, even though he couldn't see her face.

"I'm not frowning!"

"Yes, you are. You're thinking about why you shouldn't come to New York or be here with me or the million and one reasons why this is never going to work out between us."

"I am not. Quit acting like you know me so well. It's annoying."

His body shook with silent laughter.

Mary tried to pull herself free of him, but he tightened his hold on her.

"Stop," he said. "I'm only teasing you, and the reason why you're getting mad is because you know I'm right."

"I knew you had to be too good to be true."

"Mary, sweetheart, look at me."

She looked down at him looking up at her, too handsome for his own good—or hers. "What?"

"I love you."

If she'd been electrocuted, she wouldn't have been any more shocked than she was to hear those three little words from him. "You... No." She shook her head. "Don't say that if you don't mean—"

"I mean it. I love you. I love every single thing about you. I love talking to you, laughing with you, poking fun at you—and having you do the same to me. I love your sweetness and your devotion to your community. I love your beautiful face and your soft hair and your sexy body and the absolute magic of making love to you. And more than anything else, I love that I can be completely myself with you. I love you, Mary Larkin, my Sweet Mary from Vermont."

As she listened to him, tears ran unchecked down her face. "You..."

"Love you. I, Patrick Murphy, love you, Mary Larkin." He raised his hand to her face, brushed away her tears with his thumb and brought her down for a kiss.

"Wait. Stop. I need to blow my nose!"

But he didn't stop. Rather, he kissed her so passionately, she forgot that she needed to blow her nose. Who could think of such mundane things when Patrick Murphy was kissing her after declaring his love for her with such amazing, romantic words?

"Patrick," she said on a sigh when they finally came up for air.

"Hmm?" He kissed her neck and ran his tongue over the outline of her ear, making her shiver from the desire that beat through her like a live wire.

"I..." Her throat closed around a lump of emotion that made it impossible to speak. She loved him, too. Of course she did. She'd been slowly falling for him since the day she met him, and this weekend had pushed her right over the line from maybe to definitely. So why couldn't she say so?

"Relax, sweetheart. Just relax and let me love you."

Mary dropped back into the pile of pillows and tried to shut off her whirling mind so she could focus on his soft kisses, his endlessly appealing scent and the overwhelming news that he loved her.

Sunday afternoon arrived far too soon. As the day had progressed, Patrick became more desperate to prolong their time together, knowing he wouldn't see her again for a couple of weeks, if not longer. After the weekend they had spent together, it felt like pure torture to know he'd have to go so long without seeing her, touching her, kissing her or making love to her.

She came out of the bathroom, dressed in jeans and a ski sweater that looked lovely on her, but it would look far better on the floor.

He felt like a petulant child who'd been told he couldn't play with his favorite toy for the next few weeks. Even his analogy was petulant.

Mary sat on the bed next to him. "You look like you've lost your best friend."

"She's about to leave me here all by myself."

She smiled at the face he made. "Poor baby. What time are you leaving?"

"I'm flying from Burlington to Tokyo first thing in the morning. Are you sure you don't want to stay tonight? I'd get you home in time for work." He'd been trying since last night to talk her into spending tonight, too, but she continued to decline.

"I have to get ready for the week and get some real sleep, or I'm going to be a mess tomorrow."

"You could never be a mess."

"Yes," she said, laughing, "I can and I will if I stay up all night with you again, which we would do if I stay." She leaned in to kiss his cheek and then his lips. "You need to get some sleep, too. You have a big week of travel and meetings."

"I want to cancel all of it," he said, even though he couldn't.

"I'm not going anywhere. I'll be right here waiting for you to get back."

"You are going somewhere that's hours from where I'm going to be, and that makes me very, very cranky."

"Will I still talk to you every day?"

"Absolutely. I'll call you either first thing or last thing your time. I'll try not to wake you."

"Don't worry about that. I'll be waiting for you to call."

He sat up and wrapped his arms around her, holding her tight against him. "Best weekend ever."

"It was for me, too. Are you going to walk me out?"

"If you insist on leaving me."

"I do. I insist, and you need to put some pants on."

He let her go reluctantly and got out of bed to find the jeans that'd been discarded on the floor last night. Or was it the night before? As he pulled them on, he turned to find her watching him, her eyes glittering with desire and appreciation that were an instant turn-on. "Don't look at me like that and then leave me."

"How am I looking at you?"

"Like you want more."

"If I have any more, I'll need to be hospitalized."

Patrick smiled at her witty reply. His body ached in places that hadn't ached in years. Decades. It felt good. Hell, it felt amazing. He pulled on a shirt and picked up her bag to take it downstairs even as everything in him railed at the idea of her leaving. After waiting so long to find her, the fear of losing her made him feel panicky. The last time he'd felt that level of panic was when the doctors told him Ali might not survive after childbirth. Suffice to say, it wasn't a feeling he welcomed.

He forced himself to take deep breaths, to calm the fuck down and not show her how undone he was by her looming departure. She worried about him losing interest, but he was afraid of driving her away by wanting her *too* much.

Mary went into the kitchen for a glass of water. "I put the sheets and towels in the dryer. Don't forget to take them out." Over her glass, she studied him with an amused light in her eyes. "You do know how to make a bed, don't you?"

"Yes, I know how."

"Oh good. And you remember how to fold towels?"

He went over to her, unable to stay away even when she was teasing him. Taking the glass from her and placing it on the counter, he said, "Let me give that fresh mouth something else to do besides make fun of me."

She was still laughing when he kissed her, pouring all the love he felt for her into a kiss that he hoped would sustain them both until he could see her again.

He kept one arm wrapped tightly around her and buried the other hand in her thick, silky hair, wanting to keep her anchored to him forever.

The doorbell rang, and he swore as he drew back from the kiss.

"That'll be my ride."

He hugged her, buried his face in her hair and breathed her in. "Don't go."

"You'll be back before you miss me."

"No, I won't. I already miss you, and you haven't left yet."

"I have to go."

"I know," he said, but he only held her tighter.

"Patrick…"

With tremendous reluctance, he withdrew from her.

She patted his face. "Thank you for such a wonderful weekend. I'll never forget it."

"Neither will I. It was perfect. You made it perfect."

"*We* made it perfect."

He nodded because he was too emotional to speak. When was the last time he'd been so undone? Probably when he gave Cam away at her wedding. Patrick helped Mary into her coat and opened the door to greet the driver, who was annoyingly punctual.

"Afternoon, Mr. Murphy, Ms. Larkin," Bob said. "I trust you had a nice weekend."

"We did," Mary said, her gaze fixed on Patrick. "A very nice weekend."

"Excellent." He took Mary's bag from Patrick. "I'll wait for you at the car. Take your time."

"If I took my time," Patrick said under his breath, "he'd be waiting all night to take you away from me."

"You're very cute when you're pouting."

"I'm not pouting."

"You're pouting, but that's okay. It's nice to know that you don't want me to go."

"I do not want you to go. If I had my way…"

"What?"

He shook his head. "Too much. Too soon."

"Say it anyway."

"If I had my way, I'd keep you forever."

She drew in a sharp deep breath and released it slowly.

"I told you—too much, too soon."

Mary shook her head. "No, it's not. It's a lovely thought, and we'll have to see what happens, won't we?"

"We will indeed." At least she hadn't said no. He took comfort in that as he put his arm around her to walk her out to the car. After settling her in the backseat,

Patrick leaned in so she could hear him. "I'll call you later."

"I'll be waiting." He kissed her one more time and then forced himself to stand, to close the door and to wave as they drove off. For a long time after the car was out of sight, Patrick stood in the driveway, oblivious to the cold air coming from the lake or the encroaching darkness.

CHAPTER 6

"Keep love in your heart.
A life without it is like a sunless garden
when the flowers are all dead."
—Oscar Wilde

*B*ack in the house, Patrick went straight upstairs to his cell phone. He found his assistant, Maggie, who was number three on his list of favorites, after Cameron and Mary, and placed a call, not caring one iota that it was Sunday night or that he tried not to bother his hardworking employee on the weekends.

"Hi, Patrick," Maggie said. "How was the weekend in Vermont?"

He hadn't told anyone why he was coming to Vermont, even his faithful assistant, who was also one of his closest friends after so many years of working closely together. "It was great. I need to make some changes to the itinerary for the trip."

"Um, okay… What kind of changes?"

"I want to be home in ten days rather than fourteen."

"Patrick… You know as well as I do that'll be almost impossible."

"Almost impossible is not impossible. Will you see what you can do to shorten it up?"

"I'll take care of it," she said with a long-suffering sigh. By now she was certainly used to the never-ending challenges that went with working for him, and he paid her an exorbitant salary to ensure that she'd never leave him.

"You're the best, Mags."

"Anything for you, Patrick. Have a safe trip, and I'll be in touch."

"Thanks."

Knowing he could see Mary again in ten days rather than fourteen went a long way toward making him feel better about her leaving. He went downstairs and poured himself a glass of Linc's best bourbon and took it to the window that overlooked the lake. It was so pretty here. He could see why Linc and his family loved it so much.

As he stared out the window, another thought came to him, making him smile as he considered the idea from every angle. Then he went back upstairs, taking them two at a time, so he could call Cameron. She answered on the second ring, sounding out of breath. He sure as hell hoped he wasn't interrupting anything between the newlyweds.

"Hi, Dad. We just got home from skiing, and I got your email. I was going to call you tonight."

The sound of her voice made him happy—and if she was skiing, there was no way she was pregnant. Mary was right—he had to tell Cam sooner rather than later about her family history when it came to childbirth. "You had a good time skiing?"

"It was great. Will said there's hope for me yet. I say there's hope as long as I stick to the bunny slopes."

Patrick sat on the unmade bed and listened to her tell him

about being the only student Will had ever failed to teach to ski.

"He doesn't give up, though," Cameron concluded. "Even with defeat staring him in the face."

"Your mom was a terrible skier, too."

"She was?" Cameron asked in a small voice that made him feel bad that he'd never told her that before.

"Yeah, I took her a couple of times, but she couldn't get the hang of it."

"Will!" Cameron called. "It's in my DNA! My mother couldn't ski either. It's not my fault!"

In the background, Patrick heard the deep rumble of his son-in-law's voice and then the delicate sound of his daughter's laughter. "He says that's no excuse and he's going to teach me if it takes the rest of our lives. If he wants to waste his time, I can't stop him!"

"You two are funny."

"What's up with you?"

He felt guilty for not telling her he was in Vermont, but this weekend had been for him and Mary, and he suspected Cameron would approve. She'd been hoping he'd find someone new to love since she was old enough to understand what he'd lost when her mother died. "Getting ready to leave on my trip in the morning."

"Oh, that's right. Back to Asia. How long this time?"

"A couple of weeks. I'll let you know." He didn't say anything about shortening his time overseas, because he wanted to surprise Mary by coming home early.

"Did you get the invite to Hunter and Megan's wedding?"

"I did, and it's on the calendar."

"Excellent. You'll stay for Christmas, too, right?"

"Wouldn't miss it." He'd missed too much with his daughter in the past and appreciated that she held him close regardless of his failings. She was the greatest blessing of his life, and he adored her.

"Oh good! We'll have so much fun."

"I'm looking forward to it." Christmas in Vermont had never sounded as good to him as it did this year, because he'd get to spend the holiday with the people he loved best. "I won't keep you. I'm sure you must be tired after all that skiing."

"I'm exhausted and bruised from all the falling."

Patrick laughed. "Take a hot bath."

"That's the plan."

"One of the other reasons I called is I was trying to remember the name of that friend of yours in the city who does personal shopping. You know who I mean?"

"Oh, Layla?"

"Yes, is she still doing that?"

"Yep."

"You think she'd mind helping me out with some Christmas shopping since I'm going to be gone for a couple of weeks?"

"Ah, yeah, Dad," Cam said with a laugh, "I guarantee she'd be thrilled to have Patrick Murphy as a client."

"Excellent. Will you send me her info?"

"As soon as we hang up. Have a safe trip, and call me if you get a chance."

"I will, sweetheart. Love you."

"Love you, too."

He ended the call with a smile stretching across his face. Not only had he gotten the chance to talk to his little girl, but he'd found someone who could help make sure that Mary didn't forget about him while he was gone.

. . .

RETURNING TO HER ROUTINE AFTER THE MAGICAL WEEKEND with Patrick was pure torture for Mary. The days dragged. Work that normally kept her fully engaged was suddenly boring and tedious. The book her book club had chosen didn't hold her attention, and Mildred was battling a bad cold and had forbidden Mary to come over out of fear of her catching the bug. Even the needlepoint projects that were her favorite spare-time hobby didn't interest her the way they usually did.

The only thing that raised her spirits was the euphoria of the Abbott family when they welcomed Max's son, Caden, the day before Thanksgiving, which they spent in Burlington to be near Max and the baby. Things had been weird between Max and his girlfriend, Chloe, during the final months of her pregnancy, and everyone was on edge about what would happen next. For now, though, they were focused on the baby and Max, the youngest of the ten Abbotts, who'd given Molly and Linc their first grandchild.

Otherwise, Mary was completely out of sorts, and it was all Patrick's fault, which she told him on Thanksgiving night when he called around eleven.

"How is it my fault?" he asked, sounding close enough to touch when he was on the other side of the world.

"Spending time with you makes the rest of my life look boring in comparison."

"I think that's a compliment, but I can't be entirely sure."

Mary laughed. "It's a backhanded compliment."

"See, you should've come with me since you're no good to anyone there."

"True. This is all part of your evil plan to lure me into your trap, isn't it?"

"Is it working?"

"Maybe… But it's a good thing I stayed home, because Linc is going to be out all next week. They're staying in

Burlington to help out with the baby, and Hunter, Ella, Will and Cam are heading to their friend's wedding in Turks and Caicos tomorrow."

"I talked to Cam earlier. They're so excited for the trip."

"They were giddy with excitement in the office this week. So I have to ask how you managed to have *another* gift delivered, and on a holiday, no less."

"Which one did you get?"

"A gorgeous pale pink cashmere sweater, scarf and hat that is so soft I may never take it off."

"I can't wait to see it on you—and to take it off you."

"This has to stop."

"No, it really doesn't."

"Patrick…"

"Mary…"

"I told you I'm not going to forget you in the two weeks you're gone. How could I when I can still feel…"

"Finish that sentence," he said on a low growl. "Right now."

"I can still feel you inside me."

His groan echoed through the phone line. "*Mary…*"

"I couldn't forget you. Stop sending me presents."

"No."

"Yes!"

"No."

Mary laughed and shook her head. "I don't need you to do that, Patrick."

"Maybe I need to do it. It makes me happy to imagine you getting something from me every day."

"We need a compromise. Every other day."

"No."

"Patrick! Do you *know* the definition of the word compromise?"

"Yes."

"Are you being intentionally dense?"

"Maybe."

"Ugh. You drive me crazy."

"I love driving you crazy. Will you do something for me?"

"What?"

"Apply for a passport. The next time I go somewhere, I want you with me."

"We were talking about you sending me gifts."

"Now we're talking about you getting a passport."

"I can't pick up and travel around the world. I have a job and a life and bills to pay."

"If the stars align and you're able to join me, having the passport would make it easier."

"I'll look into it."

"Excellent."

"See, that's called a *compromise*. You need to compromise on the gift issue."

"I like sending you gifts. It makes me happy."

"So you said, but we both know you aren't actually sending them."

"That's not true. I was personally involved in choosing everything you've received."

"You were? Really?"

"Swear to God. I have someone who has given me options, and I choose what I want for you. It's actually been fun imagining what you'll think of the things I sent."

"I love it all. Anyone would love cashmere and sterling silver and designer purses. But it has to stop, Patrick."

"Tell me again why that is?"

"Because!"

"Ahh, I get it now."

"You enjoy being intentionally obstinate, don't you?"

"I enjoy sparring with you."

"Will you please stop sending me gifts every day?"

"I'll stop as soon as I get home. How's that for a compromise?"

"That is *not* a compromise!"

"It is to me. I'd planned to send you something every day for the rest of our lives. So, you see, I did listen to you, and I heard what you said, and I'm doing what you asked me to."

Mary's mind had gone completely blank at his mention of the rest of their lives.

"Nothing to say to that?"

"I…"

His laughter rang through the phone, and she wondered if it were possible to actually die from missing someone so badly. In all her life, she'd never missed anyone as much as she currently missed him.

"No wonder you're so successful in your business. You're a scoundrel."

"Why thank you, sweetheart. That's so nice of you to say."

"Only you would take being called a scoundrel and a tempting devil as compliments."

"Coming from you, they're the best compliments I've ever received. I miss you. You're all I think about. I can't concentrate in any of my meetings because I'm thinking about you and counting the days until I can see you again."

"Patrick," she said on a long sigh. "I miss you, too."

"You do? Really?"

"Yes," she said, laughing. "Really. I'm having some concentration issues of my own at work."

His deep sigh said it all. "I wish you had a smartphone or a computer at home so we could FaceTime. I want to see your gorgeous face."

"There's no point to having a smartphone in Butler, and I spend enough time staring at a computer at work. I've never felt the need for one at home."

"Maybe I should send you one so I can have the pleasure of seeing you."

"Don't you *dare!*"

His low chuckle made her smile. "I should let you get some sleep, and I've got a meeting to get to."

"Thanks for calling."

"Highlight of my day. Sleep tight."

"I'll try."

"You have to hang up."

"You first."

"Don't want to."

"Bye, Patrick."

"Mary..."

"What?"

"Don't go out with anyone else while I'm away, okay?"

She laughed—hard. "I'll do my best to resist the multiple offers rolling in on a daily basis."

"That's not funny."

"Yes, it really is. Now hang up and go to your meeting."

"You first."

It pained her greatly to click the Off button on her portable phone, but she did it so he wouldn't be late to his meeting. After the phone went silent, she pulled her down comforter up around her shoulders and tried to get comfortable as thoughts of him and the things he'd said kept her wide awake.

What was happening to her and her well-ordered life at the hands of this man she couldn't stop thinking about? If you'd asked her a couple of months ago if she knew what it felt like to be in love, she would've said of course she did. She'd been in love with the man she'd expected to marry after college—or so she'd thought. Patrick was showing her that she'd known nothing about love or desire or true passion until she met him.

And what was she going to do about the many emotions running around inside of her, all of them focused on a man who lived six hours from her and ran a complex life that in no way resembled hers? How would they ever make it work?

Though he hadn't said he loved her again since last weekend, he'd been showing her every day with his thoughtful gifts, the phone calls, the words he used to tell her how much he missed her. Mary was woefully unequipped to deal with the myriad emotions he roused in her and fearful of where it all was leading. She wished she could talk to someone about it, but she was fiercely private. Cameron was the one person who could shed some insight, but she couldn't talk to Patrick's daughter about the weekend she'd spent with him, the things he'd said or what they'd done together in bed.

Dear God, the thought of that conversation mortified her. And besides, it was up to Patrick to decide what he told his daughter about them, not her. That left her stuck without anyone who knew him and knew her and could maybe tell her whether she was a total fool for letting this happen.

Molly. The thought popped into her head out of nowhere. Linc and Molly had known Patrick for thirty years, since the two men had gone to college together. Molly had always been a good friend to her, and Mary had no doubt that if Molly had insight to share about Patrick, she'd do so willingly.

After tossing and turning for another hour, Mary decided she was desperate enough to confide in her boss's wife, if she got the chance.

CHAPTER 7

"The biggest adventure you can take is
to live the life of your dreams."
—Oprah Winfrey

*M*ary got her opportunity almost a week later when she worked through lunch to make up for some of the time she'd spent staring off into space lately. She had the office to herself and was pushing through her to-do list one item at a time. Charley had asked her to input some new items into the inventory system, and Mary was taking advantage of the quiet to work on a project that required her complete focus.

Patrick was due back next week, but they hadn't talked about when she might see him. He'd said something about coming to see her, but would he come right away, or would he wait until he had a chance to get away? The not knowing was making her crazy as his gifts continued to arrive every day without fail. Yesterday, he'd sent an obscenely sexy black lingerie set made of the softest silk Mary had ever felt.

Thinking about him choosing such a thing for her had her longing for him.

Even when she thought she was concentrating on her work, thoughts of him were never far from her mind.

Footsteps on the stairs that led to the office caught her attention. She looked up to see Molly coming in and breathed a sigh of relief at the sight of her. Mary had decided earlier that if she didn't get a chance to talk to Molly today, she would call her tonight.

"Hi there," Molly said cheerfully as she stopped at Mary's desk. As usual, her pretty silvery gray hair was contained in a braid that she wore down her back. In deference to the cold, she had on a coat from the store and a knit scarf around her neck.

"Hi, Molly."

"It's cold out there today. Here comes another winter in Vermont." Her face lit up with gleeful pleasure. Molly loved winter in Vermont. "Linc's not back yet?"

"No, he and Hunter were having a working lunch at the diner."

"I can catch up to him there."

"Any new baby pictures?" Mary asked, hoping to keep Molly there long enough to work up the nerve to talk to her about Patrick.

"Of course! What kind of granny would I be if I didn't have pictures?" She pulled a small photo album from her purse and handed it over to Mary.

"He's so cute," Mary declared, "and Max's smile…"

"I know. I told Linc last night I've never seen him smile the way he does when he's looking at that baby."

"How are things with the mom?"

"Ugh, not so good. She's not really engaging with Max or the baby. He's so stressed out about it all, and so are we. It's a very difficult situation."

Mary handed the album back to Molly. "I'm sorry that's taking some of the joy out of Caden's arrival."

"We'll figure it out. We always do."

Before she could lose her nerve, Mary forced herself to speak. "Molly…"

"Yes?"

"Could I talk to you about something kind of private?"

"Of course."

"Let's go into Linc's office."

"Okay…"

Molly followed her into the office and closed the door behind them. "Is everything all right? You're not ill, are you? Your face is flushed."

"I'm not ill, and everything is all right. I… I need…" She took a deep breath and forced herself to calm down. "I need some advice. About Patrick."

"Ohhhh. I see." Molly's face lit up with glee. "Does this mean something has happened with the two of you?"

"Um, you could say that."

Molly unwrapped her scarf, removed her coat and took a seat. "Do tell. I want to hear every detail."

An image of Patrick on top of her, his cock in her mouth while he tended to her, chose that moment to pop into her head, leaving her speechless from the wave of desire that overtook her. Dear God, the man was ruining her life!

"*Whoa*," Molly said. "I've never seen you blush like that in all the years I've known you."

"Because I've never had a reason to blush like that in all the years you've known me. Until now."

Molly rubbed her hands together, her eyes dancing with delight. "I knew it! I told Linc that something was going to come of you two. I saw it at Will and Cam's wedding, and I've been *dying* to ask you if anything had happened, but Linc told me not to ask. I think he's petrified that you'll quit."

"I'm not going to quit."

"Never say never, Mary."

"I love it here, you know that. My whole life is here. I can't just…"

"What? What can't you do?"

"I can't let a *man* upend my entire existence!"

"Why not?"

"Because! I love my life. I love my job and my home and my friends and this delightful little town. I can't let a man change everything, but that's exactly what he's doing."

Molly laughed her ass off. "I've never seen you so undone. This is the best news I've heard since I found out about Ella and Gavin."

"Ella and *Gavin Guthrie*? Since when?"

"A while now, and they called us last night to tell us they got engaged. I'm so happy for her. She's crazy about him."

"I've noticed that she seems very happy lately. But Gavin…"

"I know. We feel the same way. That boy has never been the same since he lost his brother. Linc and I are keeping an eye on the situation, or as much of an eye as we can. It's not as easy as it was when they lived in our barn. We have a good feeling about those two. If anyone can help that boy to heal once and for all, it's Ella. But we're not talking about Ella. We're talking about *you*—and Patrick."

"How did this happen, Molly? I was minding my own business when he came into the office with Cameron, and my whole world turned upside down. How does that just *happen*?"

Smiling, Molly said, "The same way it happened to me the day I met Linc and felt like I'd been struck by lightning. It's the best feeling ever, isn't it?"

"I guess…"

"You guess?" She raised a brow. "What does that mean?"

"It is the best feeling. Don't get me wrong. It's just that he's him, and I'm me, and... I lack the imagination to picture what could happen with him. And he's so..."

"Charming? Magnetic? Sexy?"

Mary stared at her. "Yes, all those things."

"Just because I'm crazy about my husband doesn't mean I can't see those qualities in another man. I've always thought Patrick was incredibly handsome, and in the years since he lost his Ali, I've so hoped that he would find someone special. I love the idea of the two of you together. He couldn't have found anyone better than you."

"You're very sweet to say so, but what can possibly come of it? I've never even been to New York where he lives, and he's been everywhere. He's in China right now on business. Imagine having *business* in *China*!"

"Have you heard from him since he's been there?"

"Every day. And he's sent presents. Lots of them." Mary gestured to the pink cashmere sweater that she'd worn to work.

"That is gorgeous."

She pulled back her sleeve to show Molly the elaborate sterling silver bracelet he'd sent two days ago.

"He's wooing you."

"He's driving me crazy!"

Molly laughed. "So I see."

"Let me ask you something..."

"Anything you want."

"You know Patrick, and you know me. Where do you see this going?"

"I don't know. Only you and he can know that."

"That doesn't help," Mary said, making a face. "How will we ever make his life fit mine or mine fit his?"

"That's another thing I can't tell you, but I'll point you in the direction of Will and Cameron and Colton and Lucy as examples of two instances in which separate worlds were melded with great success."

"Because Cameron and Lucy moved here, or Lucy is here most of the time, I should say. I can't, for the life of me, imagine Patrick living here."

"Maybe he'll surprise you. His daughter is here. You're here. His old pal Linc is here. I'm sure Butler is looking better to him all the time."

"Come on, Molly. This is *Patrick Murphy* we're talking about. He'd go *mad* here!"

"If I could offer one piece of advice where he's concerned…"

"Yes, please."

"Try not to think of him in terms of who he is to the rest of the world or what he has in the way of wealth. Focus on who he is to *you*."

"He… He says he loves me."

"Oh, Mary," Molly said with a sigh. "That's amazing. Do you feel the same way?"

"If the way I've missed him since I last saw him is any indication, I think maybe I do."

"So, you've seen him since the wedding?"

Mary eyed her guiltily. "Um, maybe?"

"When?"

"I might've met him at your place in Burlington for a weekend."

"No way! I had no idea!"

"This is mortifying. He worked the whole thing out with Linc, and I had no idea where I was meeting him until I got there. When I found out who owned the house, I flipped out."

Molly rocked with laughter. "I would've liked to have seen your reaction."

"I'm sure you would've been highly entertained."

"Mary," she said, grasping Mary's forearm, "I hope you

know that our home is your home. Here or in Burlington. You're family to Linc and me and the kids. I hope you'd never feel awkward spending time in a house we own."

Moved by Molly's kind words, Mary said, "Now you're making me feel silly for freaking out."

Molly smiled. "This whole thing has you unsure of which end is up."

"Yes." Mary sighed. "It does."

"Do you like being with him?"

"Um, yes?"

"Do you like the way he treats you?"

Mary thought of the gifts, the weekend he'd arranged, the driver he'd sent, the meals he'd made for them and the daily phone calls that came without fail. "No man has ever treated me better than he does."

"I think you know the answers to your own questions, so it becomes about whether you're going to allow yourself to give in and enjoy what's happening between you."

"That's the part I'm struggling with."

"I have another question… If you never heard from him again, would you be sad?"

"Gutted," she whispered.

"Mary…"

Mary blinked back tears. "I'm such a fool."

"No, you're not. You're a cautious, practical woman who's taken care of herself her entire adult life and who doesn't need a man to make her complete. So it's a big deal to admit that you have real feelings for a man and that those feelings could upend your orderly, practical life."

"Thank you for understanding something I don't get myself."

"It's not all that complicated from the outside looking in. From your perspective, I'm sure it looks extremely complicated."

"It does. I just keep getting in deeper, which I never intended to do, but he's so hard to resist. I feel like I've been taken over by aliens or something."

"You've fallen in love with an extraordinary man, and it sounds like he's fallen, too. I have no doubt that you'll figure it out."

"What if we don't and it doesn't work out? What'll I do then?" Mary ached from head to toe at the thought of never seeing him again or having something come between them.

"I'm going to predict that you aren't going to have to worry about it ending. If you ask me, your much bigger issue is going to be what to do about it *not* ending."

CHAPTER 8

"There are two great days in a person's life—the day we are
born and the day we discover why."
—William Barclay

*E*arly the next week, Mary sat at her desk sorting
through the deluge of mail that came into the office
every day. The crew had returned from the Caribbean with
the huge news that Ella and Gavin were engaged. Mary had
never seen Ella so happy or excited. Hearing how hard Ella
had fought for love left Mary feeling anxious about her own
situation. Would she and Patrick ever have the kind of happi-
ness that Ella and Gavin now had?

Thankfully, the mail arrived after lunch, when she
welcomed a more "mindless" task so she could let her mind
wander. She couldn't wait to get home to check her own
mail, to see if anything special had arrived in her absence.
And yes, she wasn't proud that she'd gotten so used to the
daily gifts from Patrick that she'd begun to actively look
forward to them and had given up on trying to get him to
stop sending them.

73

Yesterday, she'd received the most incredible pair of boots made of the softest leather she'd ever felt. The note inside had said, "Yes, I picked these out all by myself in Tokyo. So there. Miss you like crazy. Love, Patrick." When she wore them to work, Cameron, Ella and Charley had gone crazy over them, asking where she'd gotten them. "They, ah, were a gift from a friend."

"Must be some kind of friend," Cameron had said. Her knowing smile had Mary wondering if she suspected something was up between Mary and her father. She would have to ask Patrick if he'd talked to his daughter about her when he called later.

Speaking of Cameron, she came up the stairs from the store carrying her camera and a napkin that contained two of the cider doughnuts they served in the store, one of which she gave to Mary. The smell made her mouth water. "You are evil, but thank you."

"I feel less guilty if I don't eat alone."

A loud roar overhead rocked the building and had both women looking up. The only other time she'd heard a roar quite like that—

"Oh my God!" Cameron said. "That's my dad! What's he doing here?" She ran for the stairs while Mary remained riveted to her desk chair.

What *was* he doing here? He wasn't supposed to be home for days yet. What did it mean that he had come without telling her? Was he here to see her or Cameron? She took a deep breath and was letting it out when Linc came out of his office.

"What the hell was that?" he asked.

"Cameron seems to believe it was her father arriving in the chopper."

"That's a nice surprise for her."

"Yes," Mary said, swallowing hard. She didn't know what

to do. Did she go out to see him or wait to see if he came to her? And if he did come to her, how would she hide how happy she was to see him from Cameron and Linc? She waited a long time, but Cameron never returned to the office, and there was no sign of Patrick either.

Mary left the office at six and did a few errands on the way home, making sure to drive past the open town green where Patrick's big black Sikorski helicopter with the PME initials on the side was still parked. Where was he, and why did her heart beat so frantically at the thought of seeing him?

She went home, made dinner, cleaned up, took a shower and got into her pajamas, another flannel pair, this one with Christmas trees all over them. And still she waited...

In bed just after nine o'clock, she heard the helicopter take off, and her heart fell. He'd *left* without seeing her? Mary had no idea what to make of that. How could Patrick be in her town and not see her after weeks of phone calls and gifts and...

The disappointment crippled her, bringing tears to her eyes that enraged her. Mary Larkin did not *cry* over men, and she wasn't about to start now. She'd taken her book to bed and was forcing herself to concentrate on the story when a knock on the door had her flying out of bed.

She threw open the door, and there he was. Wearing a navy-blue jacket over a light blue dress shirt and faded jeans, no one had ever looked better to her than he did.

He wrapped an arm around her waist and lifted her into a tight hug. "Ahhh, there you are. Now I can breathe again."

Mary held on just as tightly to him, thrilled and relieved to see him after hours of uncertainty. "Where've you been all this time? I heard the chopper leave. I thought—"

"You thought I'd left without seeing you? Really?"

"What was I supposed to think when the chopper left?"

"How about that I sent the chopper away tonight so

everyone would think I left after a nice visit with my daughter and son-in-law."

"Oh," she said on a long exhale.

He released her and framed her face with his hands, seeming to drink her in. "I assume you still don't want Cameron, Linc or the others to know about us?"

"I… I don't know what I want."

"I know what I want," he said meaningfully, kicking the door closed and bringing his lips down on hers for the softest, sweetest kiss of her life. "As much as I love any chance to see Cam and Will, it was pure torture being so close to you and having to wait to see you."

"It was pure torture knowing you were here and not being sure I would see you."

"Let me set your mind at ease, Sweet Mary. Any time I'm here, you *will* see me." He waggled his brows. "You'll see all of me. If you want to, that is."

"I want to." She rubbed shamelessly against him. "I really want to."

Groaning, he cupped her ass and said, "Hold on to me," as he lifted her in a move right out of the best romantic movies. "Where's your room?" he asked as his lips left a trail of fire on her neck.

"That way." She pointed to the hallway off the living room. "Last door on the left."

He put her on the bed and came down on top of her, gazing at her for the longest time.

Mary raised her hands to comb her fingers through his hair and caress his face. "I missed you."

"I missed you, too, although that's not a big enough word to describe it. I was desperately lonely without you."

"Me, too," she said. "Except for the hour I got to talk to you every day."

"The highlight of long, boring days without you. Next time, you have to come with me."

"Next time, I might let you talk me into that."

"Did you apply for a passport?"

"Yesterday."

His big smile made his handsome face so much more so. Mary could look at that smile—and that face—for hours and never get enough. "You have me thinking about all sorts of things that it's far too soon to think about."

"Like what?" He made her breathless with more kisses to her neck.

"Like how I can convince you to move to New York to live with me and sleep with me every night and travel the world with me."

Mary shuddered, as much from his words as the emotion she heard behind them. The thought of such a life over-whelmed—and intrigued—her. If he were there, showing her how to navigate his world, it might not be as daunting as it seemed. "You make it sound so simple."

"It could be. If we both want the same things."

"You're right about one thing."

"What's that?"

"It's far too soon to be talking about any of this."

"I know, but being away from you for ten long days gave me far too much time to think about you and how I can have more of you."

Her heart beat fast, adding to the breathlessness his kisses had caused. And then he began to unbutton her pajama top, and she stopped breathing altogether. When he had her unbut-toned, he took the time to remove his jacket and toss it on the floor before he opened the front of her top to reveal her breasts.

"Mmm," he said, "even prettier than I remembered."

Mary couldn't breathe or speak or do anything other than

wait to see what he'd do next. She wanted to unbutton his shirt and get her hands on his muscular chest, but she couldn't seem to make her hands—or anything else—move.

He bent his head and tugged her left nipple into his mouth, sucking and licking and drawing a keening moan from her. That was all it took to set her body on fire for him. "Imagine," he whispered against the tight tip of her breast, "*this* any time we want it. Morning, noon or night, or all of the above. If I had you, Sweet Mary, I'd have everything."

Swept away by his words and his lips and his gentle caresses, Mary still couldn't believe that this extraordinary man felt that way about her.

"Tell me how you feel," he said.

"Amazed."

"By?"

"You. This. Us."

"I'm right there with you. I never expected to come to my daughter's wedding and find you, but I'm so glad I did. Tell me you're glad, too, Mary."

"I am. Of course I am."

He drew her pajama pants and panties down her legs and discarded them, looking his fill at her naked body while he dealt with his own clothes. And then he was on top of her, surrounding her with his appealing scent as well as the heat of his body joining with hers.

"I want to kiss you everywhere, but more than anything, I need to be inside you." He pressed his fingers to her core. "Are you ready for me, Mary?"

"I've been ready since the day I last saw you."

"God, you make me crazy." He took his cock in hand and worked it into her, giving her a little at a time, letting her body adjust before giving her more.

Mary clung to him, her hips rising to meet him.

"Yes," he whispered against her neck. "Just like that. God, I love being inside you."

She loved it, too. She loved the closeness, the tight fit, the heat they created together, and more than anything, she loved the way he looked at her when he made love to her.

He picked up the pace, his fingers digging into her bottom cheeks as he moved in her, his chest hair abrading her nipples and adding to the sensory overload.

"Mary," he said, sounding tense. "Tell me what you need."

"Harder," she said without hesitation.

And he gave it to her, sparking the orgasm that had hovered just out of reach.

He shouted as he came with her, driving into her over and over again until his body went slack above her.

Mary wrapped her arms and legs around him, wanting to keep him close for as long as she could.

"Tomorrow morning," he said after a long silence, "you're going to drive me to a place outside of town to meet the chopper, and then on Friday, I'm going to pick you up there after work and bring you to New York for the weekend. This is where you say, 'Yes, Patrick, that sounds like a fine idea.'"

Mary smiled against his shoulder. "You're very bossy. You know that?"

"I've been told that a time or two." He raised his head to look down at her. "Now tell me what I want to hear."

"Yes, Patrick, you bossy pain in the butt. I'll drive you to meet your fancy chopper in the morning, and I'll meet you there on Friday, too."

He gave her a light pinch to the bum that made her startle.

"What was that for?"

"If you're going to call me a pain in the butt, I figured I ought to *be* a pain in the butt."

"You were a pain in the butt long before that."

"You love me. You're just not yet ready to admit it to yourself—or me. But you will."

"You're very confident."

"I've been told that, too. In this case, I'm not confident so much as certain that we have a great thing here, and it's only going to get better. I can't wait to show you my home and my city."

"I'm looking forward to seeing it. But the helicopter part is a bit daunting."

"You'll love it. It's so much quicker than driving."

"But it's a *helicopter*, Patrick. They fall out of the sky and crash all the time."

"Don't be silly. *My* helicopter isn't going to fall out of the sky or crash. I've got the best pilots in the world working for me. And I'll be there to hold your hand and keep you safe."

"Promise?"

"Yes, I promise I'll always be there to hold your hand and keep you safe."

He made her heart race with excitement and anticipation and a tiny bit of fear over the major changes she might have to make to keep him in her life. But she didn't have to think about any of that when she had an entire night to spend in Patrick's arms.

CHAPTER 9

"Your time is limited so don't waste it living someone else's life. Don't let the opinions of others drown out your own inner voice. Have the courage to follow your heart and intuition."
—Steve Jobs

*P*atrick woke Mary before dawn with kisses down her back that had her immediately ready for more of what she'd already had twice during the night. She'd be sore and achy after another sexual marathon with him, but she'd worry about that later, after he was gone. Right now, she had enough to think about with him kissing and touching her and starting the fire burning all over again.

"Sweet Mary," he whispered. "I hate that I have to leave you today, even if it's only for a couple of days."

"I wish you didn't have to go."

"I do, too, but I've got meetings on top of meetings today." He continued to ignite her body with kisses and soft caresses of her back and bottom that had her pressing back against him, looking for more. "This is the most important meeting I'll have all day."

Mary smiled and then moaned when he reached around her to grasp her breasts, dragging his thumbs over the tips. *"Patrick..."*

"What, love?"

"You're making me crazy."

"For what?"

"You know."

"And still I want to hear you say it."

"You love to embarrass me, don't you?"

"I love everything with you. Especially this." With his hands still on her breasts, he moved them so she was face-down and he was behind her, his cock nudging at her in teasing strokes that made her even crazier.

"Make love to me, Patrick. Please make love to me."

"So polite and so sweet," he said as he gave her what she wanted in one long, deep stroke that triggered the orgasm that had been forming since she first felt his lips on her back. "I want to start every day of the rest of my life just like this."

The emotional punch of that statement had her heart expanding to the point of pain, the best kind of pain, the kind that demanded your full attention. God, she was in deep with him and getting in deeper every minute that she spent with him. When she accepted Patrick's invitation to dance at Will and Cam's wedding, she'd certainly never expected to be facedown in her bed having doggie-style sex with him.

That thought made her laugh.

"What the hell are you laughing at?" he asked on a low growl that made her laugh harder. "You're doing a number on my ego, sweetheart."

"Sorry," Mary said weakly. "It's not you."

He withdrew from her, making her moan from the loss, and helped her turn over, brushing the hair back from her face. "What is so funny?"

"I was thinking that I never expected to be facedown in

my bed doing it doggie style with you when you asked me to dance at the wedding."

His smile lit up his face. "I certainly never expected any of this, but when Cam took me up to see her office, there you were." He looked down at her naked body. "And here we are." Taking himself in hand, he entered her again.

Mary arched her back and raised her hips, wanting to get as close to him as she could.

He reached below her to grasp her bottom and hold her open for his possession.

That was the only word that could accurately describe making love with Patrick. He possessed her, body and soul.

"God, Mary... It's so good. I love making love to you. Tell me you love it, too."

"I do, I love it." She'd never loved anything more than she loved being with him this way, having him in her home and in her bed. It felt right, until she remembered the life he led far away from her little home in Vermont.

"What?" he asked, kissing the furrow between her brows. "What're you thinking that made you frown?"

"About how far from me you live."

"It's just geography, sweetheart." He nuzzled her neck, making her body tingle in anticipation of the orgasm that rolled through her in waves rather than the usual explosion. This one went on for what seemed like an hour, pleasure on top of more pleasure until she all but drowned in it.

She resurfaced to Patrick's arms wrapped around her, his face buried in the curve of her neck and their bodies quaking with aftershocks.

"Mary," he said, his warm breath setting off goose bumps on her arm. "I know you're not ready to talk about where this is going, but you have to know I'm so in love with you, and I hate that I have to leave you again."

"I love you, too, Patrick."

His head came whipping up, the expression on his face priceless and one she wanted to remember forever. "You do? Really?"

"Yes, really."

He smiled like a giddy little boy.

Mary curled her hand around his neck and brought him down for a kiss that started out soft and sweet but quickly took off from there.

Groaning, he turned his face to end the kiss. "I have to go."

"And I have to let you."

"This weekend, we're going to talk about where this is going, you hear me? We're not kids, Mary. If we both want this, and I sure as hell do, there has to be a way to make it work."

"We'll talk about it," she said, even though the thought of upending her well-ordered life filled her with trepidation, even if the upheaval meant more time with him.

"Take a shower with me."

"I thought you had to get going."

"I do."

"Showers together take more time than you have."

He gave her hand a playful tug. "I own the company. They'll wait for me."

Mary let him help her up and followed him into the shower, where sure enough, they spent half an hour wrapped up in each other's arms, kissing and touching and generally driving each other crazy with desire. "I feel like a teenager in the throes of first love or something," she said as they dried off.

"I'm right there with you." He leaned in to steal another kiss, making Mary wince from the contact against her swollen lips.

"The whole office will know what I've been doing."

"Do you care if they know?"

"I'm not sure how to feel about that, especially because I work with your daughter and you haven't said anything to her yet."

"Only because we agreed we wanted to enjoy some time to ourselves before we went public."

"I'd like to do that for a while longer, if it's okay with you."

"Whatever you want is fine with me, although at some point, I would like to tell Cam, even if she won't approve."

"Why do you say that?" Mary asked, genuinely shocked and slightly hurt. "I thought she liked me. I love her."

Patrick flashed that irrepressible grin as he buttoned his shirt. "She adores you. It's me she has the problem with."

"I don't follow." Mary pulled on yoga pants and a fleece to drive him to meet his chopper.

"My track record with women since my wife died has been... How shall I put this? Less than stellar. Cameron will be afraid of me being cavalier with you, which she has every good reason to think based on what she's seen over the years. But what I know that she doesn't, is that this is different. It has been from the beginning."

"How is it different?"

He came to her, put his hands on her hips and drew her in snug against him. "You want actual examples?"

Mary nodded.

He appeared to give that some considerable thought while his fingers slid under her fleece in search of skin. "The first time I ever saw you, that day in the office before the wedding, I thought, wow, she's beautiful. I asked Cam about you, and she said I was to keep my hands and everything else far away from you. We all know that I never do what I'm told." Nuzzling her neck again, he continued. "And then when we spent most of Cam's wedding day together, I realized you were different because I didn't want to stop talking to you. I still don't. When we're apart, I count the minutes until I can talk to you again. It's never like that for me. Usually, I'm looking for a way out from the minute I get involved with someone."

"Were you involved with someone when you met me?"

"Um, maybe?"

"Which is it? Yes or no?"

"Yes."

"Who was she?"

"Lena, my housekeeper."

"Your *housekeeper*? Does she still work for you?"

"Maybe?"

"Patrick! Does she *live* in your house?"

"Possibly? But I'm never there. You know that."

"So your ex-girlfriend-slash-housekeeper still lives with you, and your current girlfriend, or whatever I am, is supposed to be *fine* with that?"

"Mary, sweetheart, Lena and I were a fling, and we both knew it. You and I are the real thing. There's no comparison. Lena is very good at her job. She makes my life easier by taking care of a million little things that I'd never think to do, but if you want her gone, I'll let her go today."

"No! I don't want someone to lose their job because of me."

"I'd give her a very generous severance. She'd be fine."

Mary shook her head, even as unease clawed at her. "Don't fire her because of me."

"How about I find her another place to live?"

"You would do that?"

"If it would make you more comfortable with me continuing to employ her, then yes, I'd happily do that."

"I could live with that."

"Then that's what I'll do."

"Why are you grinning like a fool?"

"Because I absolutely *adore* jealous Mary."

"I am *not* jealous! Tell me what woman *in the world* would put up with that arrangement and have nothing to say about it?"

"You are jealous," he said with more of those intoxicating kisses to her neck, "and it's very, very sexy."

Mary tried and failed to push him away. The next thing she knew, they were falling back onto her bed in a tangle of arms and legs. Naturally, when they landed, his hard cock was pressed against the V of her legs. He was nothing if not insatiable. "I thought you had to go."

"I do," he said, gazing down at her with those gorgeous eyes that got to her every time he looked at her that way. "But I can't leave you with any doubts about who I'm in love with and who I am *not* in love with and never was."

"I believe you."

"You're sure?"

Mary nodded. "Are there other women who work for you that you've slept with?"

Seeming amused, he shook his head. "Lena is the only one."

"And I won't be running into her when I go to New York with you this weekend?"

"You won't see her. I promise."

"Then we're good."

"You'd tell me if we weren't?"

"I'd tell you."

"I want to get this right, Mary. Don't let me screw it up. Okay?"

"If you got it any more right, I wouldn't be able to walk, and I'd have to find a second house to keep all the presents you've given me."

"I want you to be happy. I want to make you happy."

"You do. You make me happy and silly and giddy and crazy and maybe just a tad bit jealous."

"Ah-ha, I knew it!"

"Don't gloat. It's not attractive."

He laughed—hard. "I do love you, but I have to go before they toss me out of my own company."

"You're the one who tackled me."

"Because I want one more kiss, and make it a good one to last me until Friday."

Mary wrapped her arms around his neck and gave him what he wanted, and just like always, they had to drag themselves up and off the bed and out of the house before they got carried away. She drove him to a location thirty minutes from Butler to meet the chopper that was already waiting in a big field. "How'd you find this place?"

"I have no idea. The pilots found it when I told them I needed them to pick me up outside of Butler, but somewhere drivable, so it wouldn't be too far for you to go. You'll meet me here on Friday afternoon?" When she nodded, he said, "I'll let you know what time later in the week."

"What do I do with my car?"

"You can leave it here. My people made an arrangement with the property owner."

"You have people who take care of everything for you."

"Well, yes, I guess I do. That frees me up to do what I do best."

"Which is?"

"Make money." His big smile softened the statement and made her smile along with him.

"You're very cute when you're being cocky."

"It's not cocky when it's the truth. If you want me to have a look at your retirement accounts—"

"Go to work, Patrick." She gave him a gentle push toward

the chopper, where the pilots seemed to be making a point not to look at them.

"Kiss me good-bye."

"I already did."

"I can't remember that kiss, so you'd better make this one memorable."

"You do too remember that kiss, and all my kisses are memorable."

"Damn straight they are, and I can never get enough of them." With his arms around her waist and his overnight bag slung over his shoulder, he stared at her for the longest time.

"What?"

"I haven't left you yet and I already miss you."

"I already miss you, too." She went up on tiptoes to kiss him, taking pains to make it memorable, and loved the dazzled look in his eyes when she finally released him.

"You'll be here Friday, right?" he asked with an endearing hint of vulnerability in his tone.

"I'll be here."

"Tell me again. What you said earlier... I want to hear it again."

She crooked her finger to bring him down to her. "I love you, Patrick."

"I love you, too."

"You're not going to get yourself killed in that thing, are you?" she asked, eyeing the chopper with trepidation.

"Nah, it's perfectly safe."

"Email me when you land?"

"Yeah, baby, I'll do that." He stole another quick kiss and took off toward the chopper, leaving her bereft without him, which made her feel ridiculous. They'd had hours together. She'd see him again in a few days, and yet she had a giant pit in her stomach watching him climb aboard the helicopter.

The pit only deepened when the engines fired up and the big blade on top began to spin.

As the chopper lifted off, Patrick waved to her through a small window.

With her heart in her mouth, Mary returned his wave and watched the chopper until it was out of sight, leaving behind a startling quiet that served as a metaphor for life without Patrick. It was as if he'd taken all the sparkle and color with him when he left. She thought about that on the way back home, where she got ready for work, made her lunch and went through her usual routine with a growing awareness that life as she knew it was over, and a new life with Patrick had begun.

She just wished she knew how they were going to manage that new life.

AFTER WATCHING MARY DISAPPEAR FROM VIEW, PATRICK SAT back in his seat and closed his eyes. It got harder to leave her every time he had to do it. To say his feelings for her had been unexpected would be the understatement of the decade. He'd been bowled over by her from the first time he laid eyes on her in the office, the day Cam took him up to see where she worked.

He'd only ever had that reaction to one other woman, and right when he'd accepted that he'd never fully recover from losing his wife so suddenly and tragically, along came Mary to show him he was still capable of truly loving a woman. Running his hands over his face, he tried to shake off the cobwebs of the mostly sleepless night and shift his focus to the meetings that awaited him in New York.

But he found his thoughts returning to her over and over, thinking and rethinking the dilemma of her living in Vermont while he resided in New York. In truth, it wasn't much of a dilemma. They were both adults and could do anything they wanted, but he already knew her well enough to know that she'd never go for being dependent upon him financially.

Unless he married her.

Maybe then she'd consent to letting him take care of her.

The thought had him riveted to his chair, every cell in his body on high alert. After he lost Ali, he'd vowed to himself that he would never marry again out of respect to her memory and the love they'd shared. He'd made that vow thirty years ago, before he knew just how lonely he'd be without her.

A parade of women had marched through his life—and Cameron's—a fact he wasn't at all proud of. After meeting Mary and falling in love with her, he realized he'd been stumbling through one meaningless encounter after another, looking for something he couldn't have described until he found it.

Her.

He'd been looking for his sweet, sweet Mary.

But was he prepared to marry her to have her in his life every day? Yes, absolutely. Awareness of what he'd just acknowledged swept through him like a tsunami, filling every part of him with excitement and anticipation and relief. He was so damned relieved to have her in his life, to feel that connection he'd had only one other time and to know that she felt the same way about him.

It was far too soon for his skittish Mary for talk of engagements or weddings, so he'd spend the next few months showing her she could count on him, that what they'd found together would last the rest of their lives and that he couldn't wait to have her with him every day as his wife, his lover, his best friend, his travel companion and as a stepmother to his beloved daughter.

He hoped that once Cam realized that he truly loved Mary, she would be thrilled to welcome Mary into their family. She adored Mary, and she'd always hoped he'd find someone who could make him happy while calming the restless energy that had driven him to the heights of his profession even if his personal life had been somewhat of a mess.

As the New York skyline came into view, he decided he'd take it slow and convince Mary one day at a time, one weekend at a time, one minute at a time that they belonged together. And when the time was right, he'd ask her to spend the rest of her life with him. In the meantime, he needed to see about a one-of-a-kind ring for the one-of-a-kind woman who would wear it.

By the time the chopper touched down on the roof of the PME headquarters building in Midtown Manhattan, Patrick had a plan.

CHAPTER 10

"Choose a job you love, and you
will never have to work a day in your life."
—Confucius

*D*ays had never dragged along more slowly than they did now that Mary had something to look forward to. By the time Friday afternoon rolled around, she had worn herself out thinking about him, missing him, wondering what their weekend would be like, staying up late talking to him and coming up with excuses for her friends about why she would be out of town again this weekend.

A ski trip with her college friends was on the docket for this weekend, or so she told people who asked, like Mildred Olsen. "My, my," Mildred said on Thursday when Mary checked on her. "You have been running all around lately. If I didn't know better, I'd think you have a boyfriend." This was said with a mischievous smile and a twinkle in her eye.

"Maybe I do," she said before she could take a minute to ponder the implications.

"Do you?" Mildred asked, scandalized.

"I'll never tell," Mary said with a wink.

"Well, well, well. Who is he?"

"It's new," Mary said. "I'm not really ready to talk about it yet."

"Fair enough," Mildred said, "but when you are, I'd love to hear about him. Whoever he is, I hope he knows what a lucky man he is to have caught the interest of such a sweet girl."

"That's very nice of you to say."

"It's true," Mildred said, taking her hand. "I'm so lucky to have you in my life. You're like the daughter I never had."

Mary hugged the elderly lady. "And you make me miss my mom a little less when she and my dad are in Florida for the winter."

"I hope you have a wonderful weekend with your college friends," Mildred said with a wink.

"You won't say anything to anyone, will you?"

"Never. Your secret is safe with me."

Remembering the conversation with Mildred made Mary smile as she drove to the designated meeting spot. She was on her way to meet Patrick and his huge chopper, a thought that made her giggle. How had this become her life? Her belly fluttered with nerves about her first flight in a helicopter that would take her to a city she'd never been to with a man who had become the center of her world.

They'd talked for hours about all the things there were to do and see in New York, and he'd helped her to narrow down the things she most wanted to do—a Broadway show, a trip to the 9/11 memorial, a visit to Bloomingdale's and a walk down Fifth Avenue to window-shop. If they had time, the Empire State Building and Central Park were also on her wish list.

Patrick had assured her that there'd be plenty of other opportunities to see the city and they didn't have to jam it all into two days. "We'll need some time for napping," he'd said suggestively last night, letting her know there'd be more to their time together than sightseeing.

That was fine with her. She couldn't wait to see him, to hold him and kiss him and make love with him. "You're obsessed," she said out loud, grimacing at the reality that she was, absolutely, obsessed, but in the best way possible. If this was what it felt like to be in love, she was in love for the first time in her life.

She had never felt like this with any of the other men she'd dated, even the one who broke her heart after college. That realization led to another—if Patrick disappointed her the way that man had, she might never recover from it.

No. Don't think about that. He's as invested in this as you are, and he's not going to disappoint you. Just stop.

She pulled onto the dirt road and parked her car next to the field where he'd be landing in fifteen minutes. Those last fifteen minutes felt like a week as she waited for the chopper to come into view. And then there it was, a tiny spot in the sky that got larger as it got closer.

Patrick had told her to stay in the car until they landed so she wouldn't be hit by the dust and dirt the blades kicked up on the descent. She fairly bounced in her seat waiting for the helicopter to touch down and for the doors to open. He'd told her that as soon as the door opened, she was good to go.

The door opened, and Patrick stepped down into the field. Wearing jeans and a black sweater, he looked like a regular guy. Only the huge helicopter with his company's initials emblazoned on the side gave him away as anything but a regular guy.

Mary got out of her car, grabbed her weekend bag and locked the car before walking toward him.

They met halfway, and he put his arms around her, lifting her right off her feet into a tight hug. "Longest week ever," he said against her ear so she could hear him over the roar of the engine.

Mary let him relieve her of the bag and took the hand he offered. "It was only three days," she yelled so he could hear her.

"It felt like three *weeks*." He released her hand, put his arm around her and drew her in close to him, dropping a kiss on her forehead.

The closer they got to the helicopter, the more nervous she felt.

Patrick propped his hands on her waist and effortlessly lifted her as if she were weightless. A crew member received her, helped her get settled in one of the seats and handed her a headset.

"You'll need this to be able to communicate with Mr. Murphy during the flight."

"Thank you," she said as "Mr. Murphy" took the seat next to her and donned a matching headset.

"Testing one-two-three," he said, grinning at her. "Can you hear me?"

She nodded while watching with trepidation as the crewmember closed the door to the outside world.

"Deep breaths, Sweet Mary," Patrick said, taking hold of her hand and giving it a squeeze. "I promise you're totally safe. I'd never do anything to endanger you."

She clung to his hand and his assurances as the helicopter lifted off in a great roar of noise and movement and lunging that had her gasping.

"Everything is fine," Patrick said. "Look at the scenery. It'll take your mind off where you are."

"I don't think that's going to make me forget I'm hurtling through the air in a hunk of metal."

"Then why don't you kiss me and I'll see if I can make you forget where you are."

Following his lead, she raised the microphone on her headset and leaned in to meet him halfway. The instant his lips connected with hers, she felt calmer in some ways and more agitated in others. His hand came up to cup her cheek, his thumb stroking her skin as he kissed her.

"Missed you." He moved one of the headphones and spoke close to her ear so she could hear him. "Every day felt like a week."

Mary smiled at him and reached up to straighten his hair, which had gotten mussed by the wind kicked up by the helicopter's blades.

He held her gaze for the longest time, making her feel breathless from the rush of emotion that came with sitting next to him, holding his hand and sharing this adventure with him.

Along the way, he pointed out landmarks, including the Berkshire mountains, the Hudson River and the Manhattan skyline in the distance.

"How in the world can they find where they're going in that jungle of buildings?" Mary asked as the city came into view.

"GPS," Patrick replied.

"Seriously?"

"Yep. It directs them right where to go."

"Where do we land?"

"On the helipad at the top of my building."

"You have your own building," she said with a sigh.

"You knew that."

"I don't know if I did." Thinking about the sheer scope of his life when compared to hers had her gnawing on her bottom lip.

"Don't hurt that poor lip. I quite like it."

Realizing what she was doing, Mary released her lip.

"Will you do something for me?" he asked.

"Um, sure."

"Will you not freak out when you see my building, my office, my apartment? That's just stuff. It doesn't define me."

"Doesn't it?"

"No, it doesn't. I've been worried for days about you seeing my life and running screaming back to yours. I don't want you to be put off me because of what I have. I want you to remember that I grew up in a six-room house with one bathroom that was shared by five people."

"You've never told me that before."

"Sure, I have."

Mary shook her head. "Nope."

"You promise you won't run away?"

"I promise." Mary said what he needed to hear, but butterflies stormed around in her belly at the thought of what she would see and learn about him this weekend.

THE HELICOPTER TOUCHED DOWN AT THE TOP OF A Manhattan skyscraper in a part of town full of other buildings the same size or smaller. Patrick took her bag and helped her out of the chopper the same way he'd helped her in, took hold of her hand and escorted her to a door that led to a long, dark corridor with an elevator at the end of it. He pushed the Down button, which was the only one.

"Welcome to the Big Apple," he said with the charming smile that made her heart flutter.

"It sure is big."

"It's the center of the universe."

"If you say so." She followed him into the elevator and watched him insert a card into a slot before he pushed a number. "What's that about?" she asked of the card.

"It gives me special access to the sixtieth floor, where my

offices are. I thought I'd show you where I work before we head home."

Mary felt like she'd landed in a foreign country that had its own set of rules.

The elevator doors opened to an elegant lobby with frosted glass doors with the same PME logo that adorned the side of the helicopter. Patrick used the same card to gain access to the office, holding the door for her. "After you, my love." With a hand on the small of her back, he ushered her into the office, where a receptionist talked on a headset while she typed on a computer. She nodded to Patrick, who smiled at her as they went past.

He led Mary down a long hallway full of offices with people hard at work, stopping at a desk outside of a closed door. "Mary, you remember my assistant, Maggie, from Cam's wedding, right?"

"Yes, of course. Nice to see you again."

"Likewise. Welcome to New York."

"Thank you."

"What do you think so far?"

"It's big."

Maggie laughed. "That it is. I hope you enjoy your visit."

"Thanks."

"Patrick, I put everything you asked for on your desk."

"Thanks, Mags. You're the best." To Mary, he said, "Come on in and see where it all happens." He held the door to his office for her and closed it behind them.

Mary took in the huge space with two full walls of windows that looked out over the city, the biggest desk she'd ever seen, a conference table and a sitting area with sofas and chairs. "Wow."

"Check out the view." He took her hand and walked over to the windows.

"That's close enough," Mary said, stopping him several feet from the glass.

"You won't fall out. I promise." His arms encircled her waist, and he rested his chin on her shoulder. "That's the Hudson River there and the East River on that side. Over there is the financial district, Wall Street, Lower Manhattan."

"What's over there?" she asked of the land on the other side of the Hudson.

"Jersey. That's the Empire State Building, and the one farther down is the new World Trade Center building. Look down."

"Do I have to?"

"Come on, you can do it."

She lowered her eyes to the canyons between buildings, where tiny yellow cabs were everywhere she could see.

"The roads that run north to south are avenues, and the ones that run east to west are streets. Everything is numbered in a way that makes it easy to get around."

"I'll have to take your word for that." She couldn't conceive of it being "easy" to get around a city of this size.

"By the end of the weekend, you'll totally understand the grid that makes up Manhattan." He nudged her hair out of the way and kissed her neck. "What do you think so far?"

"It's overwhelming, but I'm looking forward to seeing more."

"Maggie was able to score us tickets to *Hamilton* tomorrow night."

"Oh my God, really? I thought you said it was sold out into the next millennium."

"It is, but Maggie pulled some strings. She's good at that."

"I'm sure that all she had to do was tell them Patrick Murphy wanted to see their show."

"I told her to tell them Sweet Mary Larkin from Vermont wanted to see it. I think that did the trick."

Mary laughed. "Sure, it did."

He turned her to face him and brought his hands up to frame her face. "I need to kiss you before I die from wanting to."

"We can't have you dying when you went to so much trouble to bring me here." She curled her hands around his neck and looked up to find him gazing at her in that intense way of his. "What's wrong?"

"Absolutely nothing. I'm so damned glad you're here." He captured her lips in a deep kiss that had her clinging to him as he wrapped his arms tight around her.

Mary had no idea how much time passed while they were wrapped up in each other, the kiss going from sensual to desperate. It could've been five minutes or an hour for all she knew or cared.

He had her so close to him she couldn't miss the obvious sign of his arousal, which she pressed against shamelessly.

Patrick broke the kiss and buried his face in her hair. "I told myself I wouldn't be all over you the minute you arrived."

"If you're all over me, then I'm all over you, too."

"Mmm, I love having you all over me."

"I love it just as much."

"How about we move this party to my place, where we can be all over each other in complete privacy?"

"I'd be all for that."

Smiling at her choice of words, he stole another quick kiss before releasing her to retrieve some things from his desk. "Let's get out of here."

In the outer office, Maggie said, "You guys have a nice weekend."

"We will," Patrick replied with a wink for Mary. "I'm not available for any reason. I'll check my email once a day, so if there's a crisis, tell them to email me."

"Will do. I've already let the department heads know you're off the grid for the weekend."

"You see why I love my Maggie?" he asked Mary.

"Absolutely. It was nice to see you again, Maggie."

"You, too, Mary. I hope you love New York."

Patrick kept his hand on her back as they walked back to reception, past offices that were mostly dark. "Quitting time on a Friday," he said.

"I love Fridays. My favorite day of the week."

They rode the elevator to the lobby. "Better than Saturday or Sunday?"

"Uh-huh. I love looking forward to the weekend, even though I enjoy my job and the people I work with. It's never a burden to be there."

"That reminds me of one of my favorite sayings. Do what you love and you'll never work a day in your life."

"I like that, and it's very true. Do you still love what you do?"

"Most of the time, except when it takes me away from certain people for days or weeks at a time. I don't love it then." He carried her bag on his shoulder and held her hand as they walked through the lobby to the street, where a black Mercedes sedan awaited him at the curb.

The driver opened the back door for them. "Afternoon, Mr. Murphy, ma'am."

"Afternoon, Sam. This is my friend Mary. She's visiting from Vermont."

"Pleased to meet you," Mary said, shaking hands with Sam.

"Likewise, ma'am."

When they were settled in the backseat and Sam in the driver's seat, Patrick asked him to take them home.

"Yes, sir. Traffic is the usual Friday afternoon beast, but I'll get you there."

"I have faith in you, Sam."

"I'll give you some privacy," Sam said as he closed the window between the front and back seats.

Patrick put his arm around her. "Get over here and kiss me like you mean it."

"What does that entail?"

"Let me show you."

By the time he finished showing her what he meant, she was reclined in the seat with him mostly on top of her as one devouring kiss followed another. "Got it?" he asked.

"Mmm, not quite yet."

Smiling, he went back for more, kissing her until the car came to a halt. Patrick looked up to see where they were. "Home sweet home."

CHAPTER 11

"Change is the law of life. And those who look only to the past or present are certain to miss the future."
—John F. Kennedy

In deference to their privacy, Sam waited until Patrick opened the door and then offered Mary a hand out of the car.

"Thank you, Sam," Mary said.

"A pleasure, ma'am. Enjoy your stay."

"This is Mary's first time in the city," Patrick said as he followed her out of the car with her bag looped over his shoulder.

"Ahh, you're in for a treat, then. Enjoy."

"Have a nice weekend," Patrick said.

"You do the same, sir."

"He's so nice," Mary said.

"He's worked for me for fifteen years and still calls me sir. I've been trying to get him to call me Patrick for almost as long as I've known him."

"Evening, Mr. Murphy," the uniformed doorman said as he held the door for them.

"Hi, Gerald. This is Mary Larkin. If you could add her to my VIP guest list, I'd appreciate it."

"Will do, sir."

Patrick guided Mary through the lobby to a bank of elevators, where he produced yet another card and pressed it against a scanner. The doors opened immediately, and he ushered her in ahead of him. As if he couldn't bear to be close to her and not touch her, he slid an arm around her waist.

"What floor are you on?"

"The top two."

"Of course."

"Nothing but the best," he said with a big grin.

The elevator opened into a foyer, and the first thing Mary saw was a circular table that held a huge arrangement of colorful flowers. Marble floors, a gilded mirror, high ceilings and elaborate molding… "You have your own elevator?"

"I do. That's not a deal breaker, is it?"

"Don't be silly." She gestured to the big windows on the far side of the living room. "May I?"

"Please, make yourself completely at home. Look at anything, snoop to your heart's content, eat what you want, drink what you want. Anything and everything is all yours."

"Thank you," she said, warmed by the way he looked at her as much as the welcome. Mary wandered to the windows that looked out over the vast wilderness of Central Park. "I never expected the park to be as big as it is." In the distance, the sun dipped toward the horizon, promising a colorful sunset.

"It's about fifty city blocks in length. We'll take a walk through the park at some point."

"That would be nice. Your view is incredible."

"I'm glad you like it. What do you think of my city so far?"

"It's big and busy and hectic."

"It's all those things. It's like it has a heartbeat all its own."

"And you love it."

"Every filthy, overcrowded inch of it."

Hearing him say that reminded her of the miles that separated them in more ways than simple geography.

His hands landed on her shoulders in a gentle massage that had her leaning back against him. "I didn't make any plans for tonight so you'd have some time to settle in. What do you feel like doing?"

"What're my options?"

"We could take a walk and find some dinner, or order in and relax at home."

"Could I see the rest of your home?"

"Absolutely." He showed her the enormous kitchen, the dining room with a table that sat twelve and the cozy office where he said he spent most of his time when he was home. Then he led her to a staircase.

"I can't believe there's a second floor."

"Yep." At the top of the stairs, he said, "That's Cam's room, the guest room, and my home gym is in there." He took her hand and led her to the end of the hallway. "And this is my room."

He had the biggest bed she'd ever seen and more huge windows that overlooked the park.

"It's beautiful," Mary said, blown away.

"My daughter likes to tell me it's much too big for just me, but I like it. After growing up jammed into a small, overcrowded house, I do like my space."

Mary sat on the bed, testing its firmness. "Comfy."

He sat next to her.

"You could sleep a family of four in this bed."

He nudged her shoulder. "Tell me the truth."

"About?"

"Are you horrified by my excess?"

"No, Patrick. Your home is lovely, and it suits you."

"You really think so?"

"I do. It's larger than life, just like you."

"I want you to feel comfortable here, like you belong here, because you do. What's mine is yours, Mary."

She raised her hand to his face and caressed his smooth cheek before leaning in to kiss him. "I'm really happy to see where you live and work."

"Most of the time when I call you, I'm in bed, so now you can picture where I am when we're talking."

Mary noticed the photos of Cameron on his dresser, from the time she was first born until her recent wedding. There was one of her with Patrick and another with Cameron and Will. "She was such a cute little girl."

"Yes, she was and still is."

"She's the sweetest person. You can be so proud of her."

"Thank you. I am. Somehow, despite me, she turned out pretty great."

"One time I admired a dress she wore to the office, and the next time she came to the city, she got one for me. I couldn't believe it."

"That sounds like her," he said, smiling. "She's a lot like her mom in so many ways. I'm always happy to see Ali in her, even if she never knew her."

"She knew her mother through you."

"I didn't talk about her as much as I should have when she was growing up. I've gotten better about that in recent years and have tried to fill in some of the blanks for her." He nuzzled her neck. "So, what do you feel like doing? Take a walk or order in?"

"Is taking a nap an option?"

He raised his head to meet her gaze. "Like a sleeping nap, or did you have something else in mind?"

"What if I wanted to snuggle with you?"

"I'd be so down for that, but only if it's naked snuggling."

"Shameless, Patrick."

"Only with you." He helped her out of her sweater and then pulled off his own. "I told myself I wasn't going to talk you into bed the first chance I got."

"Why would you make such a foolish promise that you have no intention of keeping?"

He laughed. "How do you already know me so well?"

"I pay attention." She slid her arms around his waist. "And in case you were wondering, I was hoping you'd talk me into bed the first chance you got, because I've been missing you so much since you left my bed the other day."

"Mary…" His lips came down on hers, devouring and persuading, not that she needed much in the way of persuasion.

She was so, so easy when it came to him. All he had to do was look at her in that almost predatory way, and she was all in. Whether that would prove to be her biggest mistake remained to be seen. But for now, she couldn't be bothered thinking about the future when the very pleasant present required her full attention.

PATRICK HELD HER CLOSE TO HIM AS THEIR BODIES COOLED and twitched in the aftermath of the kind of passion he'd experienced only one other time in his life. Losing that, losing *her* had nearly ruined him. It had ruined him in all the ways that mattered, until he met Mary and found his way again. If she had any idea how much he'd already given her, she'd probably run for her life as far from him as she could get.

As he dragged his hand over the smooth, soft skin on her back, he acknowledged that he was well and truly screwed in more ways than one. If she asked him to, he'd give up everything for her. Everything but Cameron, that is, but she'd never ask him for that, which was one more reason to adore her. More than one woman he'd dated when Cam was still young had suggested boarding school for his daughter. Sometimes he thought she might've been better off away at school than stuck with him and the nannies he hired to care for her when he couldn't.

Regardless, he'd been too selfish to send her away, so he'd dispatched the women who made the suggestions and kept his daughter at home with him. He'd been like a zombie in those years, fumbling through his life like a dead man walking, his heart broken beyond all repair, or so he'd thought.

Mary had shown him otherwise. He had so many things he wanted to tell her, to show her, to ask her... Patience had never been his strong suit, but he knew that rushing her to commit to things she wasn't ready for would only drive her away from him—and that was the last thing he wanted. So he continued to bide his time.

"Are you hungry?" he asked after a long silence filled with the sort of contentment he'd lived without for far too long.

"I could eat something."

"You want to go out or order in?"

"If we order in tonight, will you take me somewhere fabulous tomorrow night?"

"I already have reservations at one of my favorite places for tomorrow—and I even made them myself."

"I'm very impressed," she said, smiling as she caressed his face. "So what're our options for takeout?"

"You can literally have anything you want."

"Hmmm, what're you in the mood for?"

Patrick nuzzled her neck, leaving a fiery trail of kisses from her ear to her throat.

Mary laughed, and the husky, sexy sound of it went straight to his cock, which was already hard again for her. "*Food*, Patrick. Focus."

"I'm incredibly focused." His tongue encircled her nipple, making her gasp and arch into him. "I'm known for my intense focus."

"Chinese," she said.

He raised his head to meet her gaze.

Sifting his hair through her fingers, she said, "I want Chinese."

"We can do that." Rolling onto his back, he reached for his cell phone on the bedside table. "What's your pleasure?"

"Can I see a menu? I haven't had Chinese in ages."

He clicked around on his phone before handing it to her.

"Um, how do I do this?"

Chuckling, he showed her how to move the screen with her fingertip.

"Don't make fun of me. I can't help it that my town is a cell phone dead zone."

"I would never make fun of you."

She rolled her eyes at him. "Right…" After considering the extensive menu, Mary said, "Chicken and broccoli with pork fried rice, please. Oh, and an eggroll."

Patrick took the phone from her, did some more poking around and then returned the phone to the bedside table, reaching for her to pick up where he'd left off.

"Are you going to order?" she asked.

"Already done," he said as he kissed another fiery trail between her breasts to her belly.

"When?"

"I did it online," he said with another low rumble of laughter.

Mary tugged on a handful of his hair. "You're definitely making fun of me now."

"Maybe just a little, but don't worry. You'll catch up when you spend more time here."

"I'm mad at you." She tried to move away from him, but he held her in place with his arm banded across her waist.

"Let me make it up to you." After he'd coaxed two orgasms from her with his lips, tongue and fingers, he entered her as the second one peaked and rode the waves of her release straight into his own. This was utter madness, and he loved it. He loved her, so damned much.

The house phone rang a few minutes later. He took the call from the doorman, who let him know he had a delivery. "Send it up," he said. "Thank you."

Patrick got up and pulled on his jeans, zipping them but not bothering with the top button. "Stay put," he said, leaning over to kiss Mary. "I'll be right back."

When the elevator chimed, he was ready with a twenty for the delivery guy.

"Thanks, Mr. Murphy."

"Good to see you, Eduardo." The young man brought dinner to Patrick at least once a week.

"You have a nice night now."

"You do the same."

Patrick went to the kitchen to get cutlery and returned to the bedroom to serve up a picnic in bed. He opened a bottle of Chardonnay and poured them each a glass.

Mary sat up, the sheet tucked over her breasts, her hair wild and her lips swollen from their kisses. "What?" she asked when she caught him staring at her.

"You're the most beautiful thing I've ever seen." His heart contracted, reminding him of the other beautiful woman he'd loved, making him feel disloyal to her memory. He had to believe Ali would approve of Mary, because the alternative didn't bear consideration.

Mary reached up, attempting to bring order to her unruly hair. "I'm sure I look quite frightening."

He shook his head. "No, you don't."

They ate right from the cartons, sharing her chicken and broccoli and his shrimp pad Thai. He ate with chopsticks, while she used a fork.

"I never have been able to master chopsticks," she said, watching him.

"Lots of practice."

"It's so good," Mary said with a sigh of pleasure that traveled straight to his cock. "And such a treat. We can't get Chinese in Butler."

"I'm not sure I could live without Chinese food."

"You don't miss what you don't have."

"Yes, you do," he said meaningfully. "I do, anyway. I miss you every second I'm away from you."

"I miss you, too. I'm not sure how you've managed to make yourself so essential to me so quickly."

"*Quickly?* It's taken months to get you in my bed."

Once again, he'd given her reason to roll her eyes at him. "This has happened very quickly from my perspective."

"Oh, um, okay. If you say so." He collected the empty cartons and dumped them into the brown paper bag their order had arrived in. "Six weeks has never felt so long."

"No fortune cookies?" she asked, taking a sip of her wine.

He glanced into the bag, found them at the bottom and handed one to her.

Mary opened hers and snorted with laughter.

"What does it say?"

"'All good things in good time.' How about yours?"

"'Patience is a virtue,'" he said, sporting a good-natured grin.

"The universe is trying to tell us something."

"I don't like the universe's sense of humor."

Mary took his hand and brought it to her lips. "You want everything right now, but I'm not ready for that."

"I know," he said, looking away from her. "I'm trying to be patient."

"I need some time before I can have this conversation, Patrick."

"How much time?"

"I don't know, but more than six weeks."

It took everything he had not to groan out loud and to hide the positively *im*patient response that wouldn't help his cause.

"We're going into the holiday season at the store and the Christmas tree farm. It's a hectic time of year for me and everyone who works for the company. After that, after I have a chance to catch my breath, we can talk again about what happens next."

He could wait until after the holidays, or so he told himself. "If that's what you want, sweetheart, then that's what we'll do. But I want you to promise me something in the meantime."

"What's that?"

"I want you to promise me that you'll think about the possibility of moving here to live with me and travel with me and *be* with me every day. Can you do that?"

"I'm not sure how I'll think of anything else."

It wasn't the commitment he wanted, but it was a step in the right direction.

CHAPTER 12

*"The most important thing is to enjoy your life—to be happy—
it's all that matters."*
—Audrey Hepburn

By the time Patrick and his gigantic helicopter returned her to the desolate field in Vermont where she'd left her car, a light snow had begun to fall. He'd told her before they left New York that he had to go right back to the city for an early meeting in the morning, so they had to say their good-byes standing by her car with snow flurries flying all about.

On Saturday, Cameron had called to tell her dad about Charley taking a fall off a mountain trail—on the same day Linc and Molly left for a long-planned trip to London. Thankfully, Cameron had said Charley had only injured her knee and had had surgery to repair a tear in her ACL. Mary was anxious to get home to check on her.

"Thank you for an amazing weekend," Mary said, gazing up at him, wanting to memorize every detail of his gorgeous face to hold her over until she saw him again.

"I loved every minute of it." He kissed her softly. "Will you be okay driving in the snow?"

"This dusting doesn't count as snow to Vermonters, and yes, I'll be fine."

He leaned his forehead on hers. "I don't want to go."

"You have an early meeting."

"I don't want to go."

Mary held on to him longer than she should have with the snow falling and the chopper waiting to return him to the city.

"I hate that I don't know when I'll see you again." He was off to the West Coast for the next week. His low moan of distress made her smile. He was too cute when he didn't get his own way.

"You'll see me when you get here for the wedding and Christmas."

"That's weeks from now. I can't bear it. Tell me you're thinking about what we talked about the other night."

"Patrick…"

"Please?"

"I'm thinking about it. I swear."

"Start the car and let it warm up for a minute. I want to make sure you're all set before I go."

Mary got into the car, started it and turned up the heat. Then she got out to see him off.

"I miss you so much, and I haven't even left you yet." This was said against her lips as he kissed her. If the ache in her heart at having to let him go—again—was any indication, she had fallen all the way in love with him.

He broke the kiss and wrapped her up in a tight embrace, holding on for dear life, or so it seemed to her. She loved being wrapped up in him.

"I love you, Mary. I love every damned thing about you. I want to be with you every day and never have to leave you like this again. I know you need time, and I'll give you all the time you need. But I want you to know how much I want you in every way that I can have you." He kissed her cheek and then her lips and was gone before she started breathing again.

Mary watched him jog to the helicopter, climb inside and secure the door. She watched as the engines roared to life, the big blades started spinning and the chopper took off, taking the man she loved away from her—again. When the helicopter was out of sight, she got into her car to drive home, feeling lonelier than she'd ever been. It was like he took all the magic and beauty and joy in her world with him when he left.

In a weekend filled with magic as he showed her his beloved city, he had given her a lot to think about.

I want you to promise me that you'll think about the possibility of moving here to live with me and travel with me and be with me every day.

His words were with her every waking moment of the busy days that followed her weekend in New York. They spoke every day, sometimes twice a day and often late in the night. He called from Los Angeles between meetings with the executives who ran his hotel group. His stay was extended after a woman was found dead in one of his hotels, and he had to do damage control on behalf of the property that bore his name. That crisis kept him on the West Coast until the police determined the woman died of natural causes.

He'd promised to come see Mary the minute he got home, but a windstorm in Vermont made it impossible to fly in the helicopter or the Lear.

Mary went to bed disappointed, having counted the days until today when he'd be back after two long weeks apart. Work and her commitments to friends, church and the soup kitchen kept her frantically busy, but not so busy that she didn't miss him fiercely.

When the phone rang at ten, she pounced on it.

"Hi, sweetheart." He sounded tired and aggravated. "Sorry about tonight. You can plan everything but the weather."

"That's one of our favorite sayings up here in Vermont. The weather is always scuttling plans."

"I can't recall the last time I was this disappointed."

"Me either, but another week won't kill us." He'd be in town for Hunter and Megan's wedding five days before Christmas and would be staying through the holiday. At some point, they were going to have to come clean to Cameron about the fact that they were together, especially if he planned to stay with Mary while he was in Butler.

"It just might kill me."

"Don't let that happen, please. One more week and then we have entire days together." She'd taken the week between Christmas and New Year's off and planned to spend as much of her vacation with him as she could. "Were you able to get some time off after Christmas?"

"Uh-huh. I told Maggie to clear my schedule and that I didn't care what had to happen to get it done."

"Don't make her dislike me."

"Are you kidding? She *loves* you. She loves that I have a real life outside of work for the first time since Cam moved out."

"Oh, well, that's nice to hear."

"How about we go somewhere warm after Christmas?"

"Like where?"

"Wherever you want. The Caribbean?"

"Really?"

"Yes, really," he said, chuckling. "Did you get your passport?"

"About a week ago."

"Then you're all set. Where would you like to go, my love?"

"I… I have no idea. How about you decide and surprise me?"

"Consider it done. Pack for the beach, and we'll take off the day after Christmas."

"I still can't believe that this is my life now. That you… That you're my life now."

"Mary," he said in that sexy tone that made her heart beat fast and her palms get sweaty. "You have no idea what it means to me to hear you say that, because the same is true for me. *You* are my life. Everything I do revolves around getting back to you."

Her doorbell rang, startling her from the lovestruck swoon she'd descended into.

"Hang on a sec. Someone is at the door."

"At this hour? Make sure you look to see who it is before you open it."

"I will." Mary put on a robe over her snowflake pajamas and went to see who was calling so late. At first, she thought her eyes were deceiving her, but then Patrick said into the phone, "Open the door, sweetheart."

She let out a happy cry and opened the door to him, on her doorstep, holding his cell phone to his ear and grinning.

He held out his arms to her, and she leaped into his embrace, wrapping her arms and legs around him as he kicked the door closed behind him.

"I can't believe your phone didn't cut out."

"I was praying it wouldn't, because that was perfect."

"How did you get here?"

"The old-fashioned way. I drove."

"You drove *six hours*? *By yourself?*"

"Yes, by myself," he said indignantly. "Contrary to popular opinion, I am still capable of taking care of myself."

"I can't believe you're here! And that you didn't tell me you were coming."

"I've waited two long, torturous weeks to see you. I couldn't wait another minute."

She kissed him with weeks' worth of desire and love and raw need. It was the first time she'd initiated that kind of kiss, and he responded with unrestrained ardor.

Without missing a beat in the kiss, they fell onto her sofa in a pile of limbs, his phone falling to the floor with a loud thud. She tugged at his heavy winter coat until she freed him from it.

He pulled at the tie to her robe, pushed it open and began to unbutton her pajama top. "Oh, the snowflakes. I've missed them so much." Bending his head, he kissed between her breasts and then down to her belly, seeming to breathe her in as he went. "I can't take much more of living this way, Mary. I feel like I'm half-alive when you're not with me."

Her fingers sifted through his hair, which had gotten long since she last saw him. With his chin propped on her chest, he looked up at her, slaying her with the overwhelming emotions she saw in his eyes. "I feel the same way."

The weeks without him had given her too much time to think and to ponder his offer and to imagine what her life would be like if she decided to take the leap. And now that he was back in her arms, where he seemed to belong, it became that much harder to picture the rest of her life without him by her side.

"Tell me again," he said. "I can never hear it enough."

"I love you, Patrick."

"You make me so damned happy, Mary. I'd forgotten what it feels like to be truly happy."

"You do the same for me. I've never been so glad to see anyone as I was to see you at my door tonight."

"Good surprise?" he asked with the sexy grin that made her heart race.

"The best."

"Are you still afraid of what's going to happen because you love me?"

"I'm terrified."

"No, Mary, don't be terrified. You're so safe with me. You own me. I'd do anything to make you happy. Anything at all. I'd even retire early and move to Vermont if that's what you wanted me to do. Whatever it takes to be with you every day. That's all I want."

"You'd retire early and move to Vermont?" she asked, flabbergasted.

"If that's where you want to be, then yes, I'd do it. Just say the word."

"You would hate it here."

"No, I wouldn't. You're here, my daughter and son-in-law are here, my friends Linc and Molly are here. I could make it work."

"I can't see you here long-term."

"Well, I see myself with *you* long-term. Where we are doesn't matter as long as we're together. I *need* you, Mary. Nothing makes sense without you. I'm not sure how that even happened, but my well-ordered life is a mess since I met you."

"Right back at you," she said with a laugh. "I have no idea how you did that to me. Everything was fine until you strolled into my office one day and tipped my whole world upside down by smiling at me."

"That was all it took?"

"That was it."

"We're not making any big decisions until after the holidays. My lady told me she needs time to think, and I respect her too much to rush her into deciding anything before she's ready. But she ought to know that no matter what she decides she wants, she can have it. Here, there or anywhere, I'm in this for keeps."

Mary took a deep breath that sounded more like a sob than a breath. "So you're basically saying I'm stuck with you?"

"Uh-huh. Any objections?"

"Not a single one." She drew him into another kiss, and after that, there were no more words. There were only more kisses, gentle caresses and pleasure so sharp and so intoxicating, it left her feeling almost drunk from it by the time he joined their bodies and made love to her right there on the sofa. The buzz continued when he carried her to bed, shed his clothes, climbed into her bed and made love to her all over again.

"This can't be healthy," Mary muttered after the second time—and her fourth orgasm of the evening. She was face-down on the bed after he took her from behind. Her orderly world had been thoroughly rocked once again.

"It's the healthiest thing you've ever done."

"Is that right?"

"Mmm." His lips vibrated against her shoulder, then moved to her spine, where he kissed his way down her back, his tongue dabbing into the groves and making her squirm with renewed desire for more. How did he do that?

"You're going to break me."

"Never."

"How long can you stay?"

"I have to leave tomorrow afternoon."

She moaned. "It's not enough."

"I could mention that offer I made that would allow us to be together every day, but we're not talking about that for a few more weeks yet." As he spoke, he cupped her ass cheek and squeezed, making her moan from the sensations that zinged through her, all of them converging in an insistent throb between her legs.

"I want to tell my daughter about us."

"I... um, okay."

"Is it?"

Mary turned her head so she could see him and nodded. "Since you show no sign of losing interest in me, I suppose we ought to tell her."

"Is that what you thought would happen?" he asked in barely a whisper, his expression stricken.

"I was joking."

"Were you?"

She turned over and raised herself up on an elbow. "At first, I worried about that. I don't anymore."

"Why... Why would you ever worry about such a thing?"

"Because! You're you, with your great big over-the-top life, and I'm just..."

He tipped her chin up, forcing her to meet his gaze. "You're just the sun and the moon and the stars and the entire universe wrapped up in one incredibly beautiful package. The more time I spend with you, the more interested I am. The more I touch you, the more I want to touch you. The more I'm inside you, the more I want to be inside you. I want to die inside you, my sweet love. Please don't ever have that thought again, because you are *everything* to me."

"I'm sorry," she said, deeply moved by his words. "I didn't mean to hurt you by saying that."

"You didn't hurt me. The only way you could hurt me is if you doubt my love for you is sincere and true and forever."

Mary closed her eyes against the burn of tears. "I believe you, Patrick." Believing in him required the greatest leap of faith of her life, but he'd already shown her time and again that he'd be worth the risk. She fell asleep in his arms, wrapped up in his love and thankful for every minute she got to spend with him.

MARY LEFT PATRICK SLEEPING THE NEXT MORNING AND PICKED up Mildred for church.

"You're quiet this morning," Mildred said as they drove the short distance.

"Am I?"

"Indeed. How is your gentleman friend?"

Mary felt her face grow warm with embarrassment when she thought of making love with him the night before. "He's good. Things are... good."

"You seem awfully burdened for a woman who has found a good man."

"My good man doesn't live here. He lives in New York City, and he's... He's very successful." The word *successful* didn't do justice to Patrick or his many accomplishments, but it was the best word she could think of.

"That sounds complicated."

"It is and becoming more so all the time."

"Do you love him?"

"I do," Mary said with a sigh. She'd probably loved him since the first minute she met him. Her reaction to him had been unprecedented and immediate.

"You don't sound happy about it."

"He makes me so happy. Happier than I've ever been."

"But you're facing a difficult decision."

"Yes." Stopped at a light, Mary glanced over at the sweet old lady who was her dear friend. "He wants me to move to New York and live with him and travel with him."

"How do you feel about that?"

"Excited and scared and uncertain and confused. When I'm with him, I want to take everything he's offering and to hell with the consequences. But when I'm here by myself in the midst of my lovely, orderly little life… I fear I'd be crazy to change everything for a man." It was such a relief to air it out with someone she trusted. "So I guess you could say I'm a bit of a mess."

Mildred laughed. "You're a woman in love with a man who wants to give her the world."

"Yes, that about sums it up," Mary said as she pulled into the church lot and parked in the spot reserved for Mildred, the parish's most senior member.

"If you don't accept his offer, are you prepared to spend the rest of your life with regrets?"

"Ugh," Mary said with a groan. "You don't pull any punches."

Mildred smiled. "Life is too short to spend it filled with regrets over chances you didn't take."

"I know. And you're right."

"Don't let him rush you into something you're not ready for. Take your time and think it through. If it's the right thing for you, you'll know it."

"Thank you for listening."

"I've hoped for so long that you would find someone who would love you and care for you the way your gentleman seems to. I couldn't be happier for you."

Mary leaned over to kiss Mildred's lined cheek. "Thank you."

She helped Mildred into church and tried to stay focused on the service, but her thoughts kept wandering to the man she'd left sleeping in her bed as she tried to figure out what she was going to do about him.

CHAPTER 13

"He who is not courageous enough to take risks will accomplish nothing in life."
—Muhammad Ali

*P*atrick woke to the smell of freshly brewed coffee and a note on the pillow.

Went to church. Coffee is on. Will make breakfast when I get back. xo Mary

The last time Patrick had stepped foot in a church had been for his wife's funeral. Her death had shaken whatever faith he might've had in the Almighty, and he'd kept his distance from God ever since. Church seemed to be an important part of Mary's life, though, so maybe it was time to reconsider his stance on the matter.

Whatever it took to make her happy, and if it made her happy to go to church, he could certainly sacrifice an hour out of his week for her.

While he waited for her, he took a shower and got dressed. He checked out the books on her shelf—mostly mysteries and biographies—and examined the photographs that were interspersed with books. Mary with an older couple that must be her parents, groups of friends and one of a much younger Mary with a guy that made him unreasonably jealous. In every photo, her smile shone brightly, her inner joyfulness on full display.

He loved that about her. It was one of many things he loved about her. He withdrew his cell phone from his pocket and called up the photo the jeweler had sent him yesterday of the ring he'd designed for her. Vincent, the jeweler, had taken his requests and crafted them into a stunning ring with an emerald-cut, three-carat diamond surrounded by a nest of smaller diamonds that continued around the band. All told, the ring was five carats of flawless diamonds, but it wasn't gaudy. It was perfect and one of a kind, just like the woman it'd been made for.

A car door closing outside had him returning the phone to his coat pocket. When Mary came in, her cheeks rosy and flushed from the cold, Patrick was at the kitchen table with a cup of coffee and the morning paper from Burlington opened to the business section.

Her smile lit up her face, and a rare feeling of absolute contentment came over him at the sight of her. It'd been so long since he'd felt the way he did with her that he'd almost forgotten what it was like.

"How was church?"

She removed her coat and hung it on a hook in the foyer. "It seemed unusually long today. I wonder why."

"I can't imagine." Smiling, he held out his hand to her and brought her down on his lap, wrapping his arms around her and breathing in the refreshing scent of her hair.

"It could be because the devil himself was waiting for me at home."

He laughed and nuzzled her neck. "Did you pray for me?"

"I have since the day I met you."

Stunned to hear that, he raised his head to meet her gaze. "What do you ask for on my behalf?"

"I ask God to keep you safe in that tin can you fly around in as well as on your travels around the world, and when I'm missing you, which is most of the time, I ask Him to bring you back to me."

"Mary," he whispered, moved to his soul by her sweetness. "Sometimes I feel like I don't deserve you."

"Don't say that." Her hand on his face compelled him to look at her. "You deserve me and you deserve to be happy, just like everyone else." Then she kissed him, and all thoughts of whether he deserved her were replaced with the burning need she inspired in him every time she was close to him.

"You know... I'd go to church with you if you wanted me to."

"You would? Really?"

He nodded.

Smiling, she kissed him. "That'd be nice." She kissed him again. "Are you hungry?"

"Mmm," he said against her lips. "Starving."

"For food?"

"Among other things."

"Which do you want first?"

"You," he said. "Always you."

Without another word, she got up from his lap, took his hand and led him back to bed.

"I HAVE TO GO SOON," PATRICK SAID LATER THAT AFTERNOON. They were still in her bed, where they'd been all day except for a trip to the kitchen to make sandwiches that they ate in bed.

Mary held on tighter to him as he ran his fingers through her hair. "Not yet."

"I'll be back on Friday for the wedding."

"That's five whole days from now."

"It'll go by quickly. And we'll have almost two weeks together."

"I can't wait. Did you decide where we're going?"

"How does Martinique sound?"

"To someone who hasn't been anywhere, it sounds divine."

"It's beautiful. You'll love it. A friend of mine has a house with a pool right on the beach. He was happy to lend it to me in exchange for a weekend at my place in Vail next winter."

"You have a place in Vail?"

"A condo. I like to ski."

"Do you have other homes?"

"Nope, that's it. I don't feel the need to collect houses, although I can stay at any of my hotels whenever I want, so it's like I have homes all over the world."

"Why aren't we staying at one of your hotels on our trip?"

He dragged his finger down her arm. "Because I want to be completely alone with you, and if we're at one of my properties, it'll turn into business for me. I don't want that. This trip is all pleasure and no work."

Filled with anticipation for the trip, Mary rested her head on his chest and sighed with contentment. The only thing that stood in the way of her complete contentment was the fact that he had to leave—again. It was becoming harder all the time to let him go, to miss him between visits, to rely on daily phone calls that were no substitute for the real thing.

"What're you thinking about, sweetheart?" His hand continued to slide up and down her arm, sending waves of sensation rippling through her.

"That I miss you and you haven't even left yet."

"That's my line."

"It's *our* line."

Patrick rolled them so he was on top looking down at her. He studied her for a long, charged moment before he joined his lips with hers, giving her sweetness and nearly unbearable tenderness as he loved her one last time before they had to say good-bye for now.

Afterward, he held her close to him while their hearts pounded in unison. "I love you so much, and I hate to leave you."

"I love you, too, and I hate to let you go."

"Five days, and then I'll be back." With one last kiss, he got up to take a shower. Thirty minutes later, he was dressed and ready to go.

Mary got up, pulled on a robe and walked him to the door. "Thank you for the best surprise ever."

Resting his hands on her shoulders, he looked down at her. "I loved every minute of it."

"Call me when you get home?"

"I'll probably want to call you long before then."

"I'll be here." She hadn't done any of her usual Sunday chores, but what did she care when she'd gotten an entire day with Patrick? If she had to go to the diner for lunch tomorrow, then so be it.

"I'm going to tell Cameron about us the next time I see her. If that's okay with you."

"That's more than fine with me."

His sexy half smile made his gorgeous eyes twinkle. "I feel guilty for being here and not seeing her."

"You'll see her next weekend. She's excited to have you here for the wedding—and Christmas."

"I told her I'm going to stay at the Butler Inn so I'm not crowding her and Will, but I hope it's okay if I stay here with you."

"I'd be disappointed if you didn't. I'll wait to decorate my tree until you get here."

"That'll be fun. I haven't decorated a Christmas tree in... Well... ever."

Mary laughed. "Let me guess, someone does that for you, too?"

"Maybe. Maybe not." He rested his forehead against hers. "Tell me I have to go."

"Patrick, you have to go."

"I don't want to."

She slid her arms around his waist and held him close.

"That's not making it easier for me to leave."

"I'll let go in a minute."

He wrapped his arms around her and held her as close to him as he could get her.

"You'll drive carefully, won't you?"

"I will. Don't worry."

"I'll worry until I hear you're safely home."

"When I call you, Sweet Mary, I'll be safely back in the city, but these days, home seems to be wherever you are." He kissed her like it was the first time all over again, and she returned his kiss with the desperation that came over her every time he had to leave. "Mmm. If I don't stop now, I won't be able to." He kissed her quickly, one last time, then hoisted his bag onto his shoulder and dashed off into the encroaching darkness that arrived early this time of year.

Mary watched him get into a black Lexus SUV with New York plates. She watched him pull out of the driveway and drive off toward town on his way to the interstate that would take him away from her. After she closed the door, she leaned against it for a long time, thinking about the offer he'd made her and realizing that with every good-bye, it became harder to remember all the reasons why she'd hesitated to jump at his offer of a life together.

Yes, everything would change, but hadn't it already? She barely remembered what life was like pre-Patrick. It was a whole lot less exciting than post-Patrick had been, that was for sure.

The phone rang, and expecting it to be Patrick, she answered on the first ring.

"Who're you waiting to hear from, honey?" her mom asked.

"I happened to be standing right next to the phone when it rang. How're you?"

"We're good. The weather is great, and Daddy is playing golf with Mr. Wilson and some other friends. I had some time to myself, so I figured I'd give you a call. I'm not catching you at a bad time, am I?"

Mary curled up on the sofa and pulled a blanket over her lap. "No, this is a good time. I had a friend here, but he just left."

"A friend or a *friend*?"

Mary took a deep breath and said, "The latter."

"Mary! Since when? Who is he? What's his name?"

Mary laughed at the barrage of questions. "Since October, and does the name Patrick Murphy ring any bells?"

A gasp preceded a sputter. "As in the *billionaire*?"

"The one and only."

"Start talking, young lady, and don't leave *anything* out."

Since Mary had been dying to tell the people that mattered to her about Patrick, she told her mom about meeting him at Will and Cam's wedding, how they'd danced and connected in a way she hadn't with anyone else in years. She mentioned the flowers he'd sent, the phone calls and her trip to New York. "We went to the World Trade Center memorial and the Empire State Building. We saw *Hamilton* and ate at the Rainbow Room."

"Oh, Mary, it sounds wonderful."

"It has been. He's amazing."

"You sound like a woman in love."

"I am."

"Mary… Now you're going to make me cry! I never expected to hear all this when I called to check in."

"I haven't meant to keep it from you. It's just that it's still sort of new, and I haven't really told anyone."

"You don't have to apologize to me, honey. You're a grown woman with your own life. It sounds like you've been experiencing a bit of a fairy tale."

"I have been."

"So if he lives in New York and you live in Vermont, how will that work long-term?"

"Patrick has asked me to come live with him in New York. He wants me to travel with him and be with him all the time."

"Oh," her mom said on an exhale. "Wow. What did you say?"

"I told him I'd think about it, and I am. I'm thinking about it." Pretty much all the time, not that she told her mother that.

"I'm afraid I'll sound terribly old-fashioned if I express concern about you giving up your life and your home and job for a man without a real commitment."

"He's very committed to me, Mom. He drove twelve hours round trip to see me for one day when the weather was too bad to fly. When he went to China and Japan last month, he sent me something every day so I wouldn't forget about him while he was gone. He told me he loves me weeks ago, and he tells me every chance he gets how much he wants me in his life."

"Does he make you happy, sweetheart?"

"Happier than I've ever been—until I start thinking about where this is heading or how he's going to change my entire life. Then I start to feel nervous and a bit panicky."

"Daddy and I would love to meet him."

"We're going to the Caribbean on vacation after Christmas. I could ask him if we could stop in Sarasota on the way to see you." As she said the words, she hoped that Patrick wouldn't mind the extra stop.

"It'd be terribly expensive to fly out of your way like that."

"He has his own plane, Mom," Mary said with a laugh.

Her mother laughed, too. "Yes, I suppose he does. This is all a lot to take in. I'm sorry if I'm not saying the right things. You took me by surprise with this big news."

"Trust me, it's a lot for me to take in, too." Mary almost choked on the double meaning behind her statement. Patrick was a *lot*, in more ways than one, but she loved him anyway. "For what it's worth, I really think you guys will like him."

"We'll look forward to your visit. Just let me know when so we can make sure we don't make any other plans."

"I'll talk to him tonight and email you."

"Do you mind if I tell Daddy your news?"

"I don't mind."

"I hope you know how happy I am to hear that you've met someone who is so good to you. You deserve it."

"Thanks, Mom. Love to you and Dad."

"Love you, too. I'll look for that email."

They said their good-byes, and Mary had a moment of panic, wondering what Patrick would think about stopping to see her parents on their way to the Caribbean. She decided she couldn't wait until later to ask him if it was all right, so she called his cell phone.

"Hi, sweetheart. Miss me already?"

"You know I do. Where are you?"

"Almost to Rutland. What're you up to?"

"My mom called, and I told her about you."

He was quiet for a moment, and then he said, "Did you now?"

"Uh-huh. She said they'd like to meet you, so I told her

133

maybe we could stop to see them in Sarasota on our way south? If that's okay with you. If it's not—"

"Mary, sweetheart, of course it's fine with me. I'd love to meet your parents."

"Oh, okay," she said, exhaling a breath she hadn't realized she was holding.

"Please don't ever hesitate to ask me for whatever you want."

"I'm still getting used to this."

"This meaning me?"

"This meaning all of it—you, me, us."

"You can have all the time you need to get used to the fact that I'm crazy in love with you and fighting the urge with every passing mile to turn around and come back to you."

When he said things like that, her heart beat so hard and so fast that she felt like she was hyperventilating. "When we go on our trip," she said, "do you think we could talk some more about what you asked me, about coming to live and travel with you?"

"Yes, Mary," he said softly. "We can definitely talk about that. In fact, there's nothing I'd rather talk about."

"Will you call me when you get home so I know you got there safely?"

"It's apt to be late."

"I don't mind."

"Okay, honey. I'll call you when I get home."

"Patrick?"

"Yes?"

"Please drive carefully."

"I will. I promise."

Mary put down the phone but kept it close by until he called around midnight to tell her he was home. "I wish you were still here with me," she said.

"You have no idea how much I wish that, too."

"I really do love you, Patrick."

"That makes me so happy, because I really love you, too. Get some sleep, and I'll talk to you in the morning."

Mary fell asleep with a smile on her face, hugging the phone to her chest.

CHAPTER 14

*"Life was always a matter of waiting
for the right moment to act."*
—Paulo Coelho

The five days between his departure on Sunday and his return trip for Hunter's wedding helped to clarify a few things for Mary. First and foremost, she wanted to be with Patrick, even if that meant upending her entire life to make it happen. She had always played it safe, and that had gotten her a satisfying if not overly exciting life. Patrick had changed everything, and there was no going back to who she'd been before him.

This week had dragged, every minute feeling like another hour she had to get through before she could be with him again. So when she heard the roar of his helicopter on Friday afternoon, her eyes filled with tears and her heart began to pound with excitement and anticipation.

She wanted to feel that way every day for the rest of her life, and she wanted to spend that life with Patrick. After the wedding and the holidays, she would tell him she wanted to move to New York to live with him, as long as he would agree to let her work so she could continue to support herself. That was important to her, and she hoped he understood that she couldn't allow him to support her, no matter how wealthy he might be.

With the office emptying out for the wedding weekend, Mary and Linc were the last ones left. She gathered her belongings and went to tell Linc she'd see him later at Hunter and Megan's rehearsal dinner at a place called The Pig's Belly, of all things.

"I'm going to head out," Mary said. "I'll see you tonight."

"I'll walk you out." He got up and shut off the lights and followed her to the stairs.

"You ready for another wedding?"

"I suppose I have to be," he said with a smile. "Hunter is so in love with that girl, and she's a doll. I'm thrilled for them, but my kids grew up way too fast."

"Remember when you thought your barn would always be full of kids?"

Nodding, he said, "And now Molly and I rattle around the empty place." Glancing over at her as they reached the bottom of the stairs, he said, "Everything okay with you, Mary? You've been quiet lately."

"Everything is fine," she said, patting his arm. Though she was tempted to tell him about Patrick, she couldn't do that until Patrick came clean with Cameron. Lincoln would hear the news soon enough. "But thank you for asking."

"Glad to hear it. I'll see you in a couple of hours. Molly tells me The Pig's Belly is an experience we won't want to miss."

"I'm looking forward to it."

They parted company in the parking lot, and Mary drove home wondering when she would see Patrick. Would he go to Cameron's or come to her first? She got her answer when she pulled up to her house and found him sitting on her front steps like it was July rather than late December. His suitcase and suit bag were on the porch behind him.

He stood to greet her, smiling widely.

She couldn't get out of the car fast enough and didn't give a single thought to nosy neighbors when she rushed into his outstretched arms and kissed him. "I thought today would never get here."

"Same. The days without you drag endlessly."

After a long hug, he let her go and followed her inside, bringing his bags with him. "I told Cam I'm staying at the Butler Inn, and I'd catch up to her at dinner. I'm going to talk to her about us after the wedding."

She took his coat and hung it next to hers. "Our little secret won't be a secret for much longer."

"That's fine with me. I want the whole world to know how much I love you." His arms came around her waist, and he buried his face in her hair, drawing her close. They stayed that way for a long time, holding on tight to what they'd found in each other. "I'm so excited to have the next couple of weeks with you. I told Maggie to only call me if the building was on fire."

"I still have to work until Christmas Eve," she reminded him. "The store is crazy busy this week."

"I'm sure I'll find something to keep me busy while you're working."

She turned to face him, resting her hands on his chest. "After Christmas Eve, I'm all yours."

"Best Christmas present I've ever gotten."

"Tomorrow, before the wedding, we can go get a tree."

"Whatever you want to do."

"We've got a couple of hours before we have to be anywhere," she said, smiling up at him.

"Whatever shall we do with all that time?"

Smiling, she took him by the hand and led him into her room.

"My Sweet Mary is full of surprises."

She lifted his sweater up and over his head, baring that chest she couldn't stop thinking about. "You've made me this way."

"I have? And what way is that?"

"Sex crazy, and yes, it's all your fault."

"I can live with that."

They undressed each other and slid into the cozy warmth of her flannel sheets and down comforter. His arms came around her, their legs entangling and his lips finding hers in a desperate kiss that told her just how much he'd missed her. "This is, officially, my favorite place in the whole world."

"In my bed in Vermont?"

"In *any* bed with you."

"It's my favorite place, too."

He caressed her cheek and pushed the hair back from her face. "I'm not going to be able to bear to let you go after having a couple of weeks with you."

"We don't need to think about that now."

"No, but we need to talk about it soon. I can't stand being away from you."

"I can't stand it either."

"That's so good to know," he said with a rakish grin that lit up his eyes.

Mary moved so she was on top of him, registering his look of surprise with pleasure. She loved to surprise him. "Can we do it like this?"

"We can do whatever you want, my love." He slid his hands from her hips to her breasts.

"No hands. Put them under your head."

"Do I have to?"

"Uh-huh. You're not in charge right now. I am."

"I've never been so happy to be bossed in my entire life."

"Have you ever actually been bossed?"

"Um, I think so. Once. When I was fifteen."

Mary laughed and peppered his chest with kisses, working her way down to the erection that reached beyond his belly button. Wrapping one hand around the base, she bent over him, loving the gasp that escaped his lips when her hair brushed against the head of his cock. Since he loved to drive her to the point of madness before making her come, she decided to give him a taste of his own medicine. She took her own sweet time, teasing him with her hands and tongue and hair.

His hips came off the bed, silently begging her for more, but still she made him wait.

"Fuck, Mary. I thought you loved me."

"I do." She drew the head into her mouth and sucked lightly, pulling a deep groan from him. "I love you so much, it's crazy. You're all I can think about."

"Baby, let me touch you."

"Not yet. I'm not done." To punctuate her words, she cupped his balls and squeezed lightly as she took him in as far as she could, using her tongue and lips to pleasure him.

"Mary!"

She heard the warning, knew she was playing with fire and didn't retreat.

"God, Mary…" His hips came off the bed, and he grasped her hair in the second before he came.

She stayed with him until he sagged into the bed, the act so personal and intimate, she felt seared in the aftermath. She'd never done that for anyone else, had never wanted to. But with him, all her walls had fallen and nothing was off-limits because of how much she loved him.

Kissing his belly and chest, she worked her way to his neck as his arms came around her.

"You are so incredibly sexy," he said.

"I've never felt sexy until you came along."

"That's a goddamned shame." He kissed her until he was hard again, and Mary took him in slowly, coming down on top of him as he dragged his thumbs over her nipples.

Patrick sat up and wrapped his arms around her, holding her tight against him as they moved together in perfect harmony.

She'd never experienced anything better than the exquisite pleasure she found with him, and the thought of a lifetime of such pleasure filled her with giddy joy.

His hands dropped to her ass, squeezing as she moved. Then he hit a spot deep inside her that triggered a powerful release for her and then him.

She sagged into his embrace, exhausted and exhilarated at the same time. If he asked her right now to give up everything she'd ever known for him, she'd do it. She'd do it in a New York minute. The pun made her giggle.

"It's not polite to laugh when a man's penis is still inside you."

"I'm not laughing at you or your delicate penis."

"My penis is not delicate, as he has proven many, many times."

"Stop," she said, laughing uncontrollably now.

"Not until you tell me what's so funny."

"I can't."

He rolled them so he was on top of her. "Tell me."

"I had this thought."

"I'm listening…"

"That if you asked me right now, I'd give up my whole life in a New York minute if I got to spend the rest of it with you. It was the New York minute that made me laugh."

His expression turned fierce. "I'm asking. Right here and now. Marry me, Mary. Live with me. Travel the world with me. Sleep with me every night. Wake up with me every morning. Be my love."

"Patrick…" Her eyes filled with tears that slid down her cheeks. "I was joking. I wasn't asking you to propose."

"I'm dead serious. Hang on a minute." He withdrew from her, got up from the bed and went to root around in his bag, returning with a black velvet box that he held out to her.

"What…" She looked up at him. "You…"

"Open it."

Mary's hands trembled as she opened the box, gasping at the sight of the most incredible ring she'd ever seen.

"I had it made for you. I was planning to propose on our trip. You just gave me the perfect opportunity." Dropping to his knees next to the bed, he reached for her hands. "Will you please marry me, Sweet Mary from Vermont?"

Without a moment's hesitation, she said, "Yes."

"Really?"

She nodded and tugged on his hands to bring him back to her. "Really."

He took the velvet box that had fallen to the bed and removed the ring to slide it onto her finger.

"It's so beautiful."

"It's not too much?"

"No, it's perfect. I love that you had it made just for me."

"It's one of a kind, like you."

"I can't believe this is happening."

"Believe it. Believe in me and us. This is forever."

"We can't tell anyone. This is Hunter and Megan's weekend. We can't steal their thunder."

"And I probably ought to tell my daughter we're together before I tell her we're engaged."

"That, too." She smiled at him.

He smiled back at her. "I'll tell her tomorrow after the wedding."

"We're really engaged?" She'd thought she felt giddy before. Now, her heart beat so fast, she feared she might pass out.

Patrick kissed the hand that now sported his ring. "We're as engaged as it's possible to be."

"And we have to act like nothing special has happened in front of everyone I know."

"Just for a little while longer. After the New Year, we'll come back from our trip and tell everyone the good news. The engagement part can be our secret for now."

"It's the best secret I've ever had."

He snuggled up to her and drew the comforter over them. "Me, too, sweetheart."

MARY FLOATED ON AIR THAT WEEKEND, THROUGH THE festivities at The Pig's Belly, when she had to pretend that she and Patrick were just friends, and the next day when Hunter and Megan tied the knot in a touching, beautiful ceremony at Linc and Molly's big red barn.

Mary stood with Patrick during the ceremony and the speeches that followed. Megan's sister Nina was toasting the bride and groom when a shout from behind them had Mary and Patrick turning in time to see Cameron land in a heap on the floor.

Will cried out in distress.

Patrick ran to her, dropping down next to his son-in-law.

Cameron came to a few seconds later, asking what happened and then apologizing to Megan for stealing her thunder.

"I don't care about that," Megan said. "As long as you're all right."

Cameron looked up at Will, a small smile occupying her lips. "I'm all right, and I'm pregnant."

While everyone else cheered the good news, Mary went cold inside, knowing what she did of Cameron's family history.

"A baby?" Patrick asked, his voice filled with wonder.

"So it seems, although this wasn't how I'd planned to tell you."

Patrick hugged her, holding her for a long moment. By the time he released her, some of the color had returned to Cameron's pale cheeks.

Will and Patrick helped her up, then Will scooped her into his arms to carry her out of the room. Mary, Patrick, Molly and Lincoln followed.

"I'm so sorry to worry you all," Cameron said. "I stood too close to the fireplace, and the heat did me in."

Molly brought her ice water and ushered everyone from the room, so Cam and Will could have a minute alone.

Patrick looked like he'd been electrocuted.

Mary guided him into the kitchen and encouraged him to breathe.

"Oh my God," Patrick said, stricken. "She's pregnant. She can't... I can't... I can't lose her, Mary. I'd never survive it."

"We'll give them a minute, and then we'll go talk to her. You can tell her what you're worried about and give her all the information she needs."

"I should've told her. Before they got married, but she was so happy... I couldn't. I couldn't do that to either of them."

Mary took his face in her hands, not giving a flying fig if anyone came upon them in an obviously intimate moment. "Thirty years have gone by since Ali died giving birth. Everything has changed since then. Cameron is young and strong and healthy. She's going to be just fine, and you, my friend, are going to be a grandfather."

"A grandfather," he whispered. "How do you feel about being married to a grandfather?"

"I may have to reconsider in light of this development. I'm still a very young woman. I ain't nobody's granny."

His mouth lifted into a small smile that was a welcome change from the sheer terror of a few minutes ago. "You're going to be the sexiest granny ever."

"Let's go talk to Cameron and put your mind at ease."

They found Will and Cam still in the den. She was on his lap, and his arms were wrapped around her.

"Sorry to interrupt," Patrick said haltingly.

Mary rested a hand on his back and sat with him on a love seat.

"You're not," Cameron said. "Come in. Sorry to cause such a scene."

"It's not your fault you fainted, babe," Will said.

"Still, I never like to be a drama queen."

"You're not," Patrick said. "You never have been."

"The best part of being pregnant is no more skiing lessons for almost a year," Cameron said with a grin for her husband. "Why do you look so freaked out, Dad?"

"I… Um… It's just… Well, I'm so excited for you guys. I hope you know that. But, um… your mom and what happened—"

"That's not going to happen to me," Cameron said adamantly.

"How can you possibly know that?"

Cameron glanced at Will, who nodded in encouragement. "Before we started trying to get pregnant, I spent two nights at Mass General, where I had a full cardiac and obstetrical workup that found absolutely no reason for concern. I'm perfectly healthy."

"You did? You are?"

"I had the same concerns, Patrick," Will said. "I insisted we make absolutely sure that having babies wouldn't be too dangerous for her. I wouldn't hear of even trying until we were one hundred percent sure. And now we are. Of course, she took five years off my life by fainting just now, but that was only because she was too warm standing by the fire."

"God, that's such a relief," Patrick said.

"I'm sorry you were worried," Cameron said with a sweet smile for her father.

Patrick glanced fleetingly at Mary before returning his attention to Cameron. "There's something you don't know, sweetheart. Your grandmother..."

"Also died in childbirth, having her fifth child," Cameron said.

"How do you know that?" he asked, sounding astounded.

"I connected years ago with Mom's sister Cindy on Facebook. She told me."

"You didn't tell me."

"I wasn't sure how you'd feel about me being in touch with her after the way Mom's family treated you."

"I wouldn't have minded. They're your family."

"For better or worse," Cameron said with a wry smile. "The specialists at Mass General said that I was wise to be tested in light of my family history, but they could find no reason to believe I have anything worry about, and they were incredibly thorough." She grimaced. "It was no fun."

"She was a trouper," Will said.

"Thank you for insisting that she do that," Patrick said to Will. "I wish you guys had told me about it."

"You were in Europe, and we didn't want you to worry," Cameron said. "And don't tell me you wouldn't have worried."

"You're right," Patrick said, smiling at her. "I would have."

"I had the same fears you do, Patrick," Will said. "I'd rather be childless than lose Cam the way you lost her mom. I don't know how you survived it."

146

"I didn't, really. I was a disaster for years, and Cameron paid the price for that."

"Now that I have Will," Cameron said, "I have a much greater understanding of what it must've been like for you to lose Mom so suddenly. I can't imagine that happening to me and having to cope with a baby at the same time. I hope none of us ever knows that kind of pain. I wish you would find a way to forgive yourself for not being the perfect dad. You were perfect for me." She got up and came over to Patrick, reaching out to him.

He stood and wrapped his arms around her.

Mary dabbed at her eyes, moved by Cameron's loving words for her father, knowing how much they would mean to him.

"I have something to tell you, too," he said.

"What's that?"

"So Mary and I—"

"I just said to Will that there was something going on with you guys! Since when?"

Patrick looked at Mary, smiling. "Since your wedding."

Cameron's face lit up with a huge smile. "Oh my God! How could you keep this secret from me when I'm the one who introduced you?"

Patrick sat next to Mary and took her hand. "We wanted a little time to ourselves before we told people, and I was a little afraid you might not approve. After all, you told me to keep my hands and everything else away from Mary the day you introduced us."

To Mary, Cameron said, "Does he treat you right?"

Mary looked at Patrick. "No one has ever treated me better."

"Then I completely approve. This is so exciting!"

"I'm glad you think so," Patrick said. "We're really happy

together. In fact…" He looked around to make sure no one else could hear him. "We're getting married."

"Patrick! We said we weren't going to tell anyone yet."

"Cameron is not anyone. She's my little girl. I have to tell her."

His little girl clapped her hands together with giddy excitement while Will looked on, beaming at all of them.

"You guys aren't going to believe what just happened," Ella said as she came into the room, looking slightly shell-shocked.

"What's up?" Will asked his sister.

"Chloe was just here," she said of Max's girlfriend and Caden's mother.

"What did she want?"

"She signed over full custody of the baby to Max. She said she's not ready to be a mother."

"Oh my God," Cameron said. "He must be freaking out."

"To say the least," Ella said.

Poor Max, Mary thought. What an overwhelming responsibility for such a young man. He'd only just graduated from college, and now he was a single dad.

"Apparently, Mom really took control of the situation, and our cousin Grayson had already prepared custody paperwork that outlined all their options. She chose to give sole custody to Max."

"Holy shit," Will said. "I need to go check on him."

"Of course." Cam stood to let him up. When she wobbled ever so slightly, he settled her back on the sofa with a blanket over her. "Don't move until I get back."

"Yes, dear," she said, smiling at him.

Ella went with Will, leaving Mary, Patrick and Cameron in the den.

"I feel for the guy," Patrick said.

"You've certainly been there, done that," Cam said.

"He'll have the support of a big, loving family all around him," Mary said. "He'll be okay."

"I want to talk about you two," Cameron said. "I want all the PG-13 details of how this went down. Leave nothing out but the gross stuff. And I take it you're not *really* staying at the Butler Inn this week."

"Busted," Mary said.

Laughing, Patrick told his daughter their story, leaving out the delicious details that belonged to them alone.

CHAPTER 15

"Life is either a great adventure or nothing."
—Helen Keller

On the way back to Mary's house, a light snow fell, making it hard to see the road or the huge moose standing in the middle of it until they almost hit him. Patrick slammed on the brakes, and the car spun around in a full circle before coming to a stop. The moose never flinched.

"Jesus," Patrick said. "Are you okay?"

"I'm fine."

"What the actual hell?"

"That would be Fred the Moose. You met him at Cam's wedding."

"I remember. Dear God, my daughter ran her car into him and lived to tell."

"And that's how she became the girl who hit Fred."

"My hands are shaking, and I didn't even hit him."

"Fred shows up in the damnedest places around here. You never know where he's going to be. Locals have learned to keep an eye out for him."

"I think I might be having a heart attack." He reached for her hand and placed it over his fast-beating heart.

"Nah, you're just having a Fred anxiety attack. But he's harmless. Don't worry. We may have to wait him out, but eventually he'll move along."

"He's a big mo-fo."

"That he is."

Fred let out a loud "moo" that had Patrick jolting and Mary laughing.

"Do *not* laugh at your fiancé. It's not nice."

That only made her laugh harder.

He tugged her closer to him and kissed her. "Quit it."

"I can't." She'd laughed so hard that tears filled her eyes.

"How long are we going to be stuck here?"

"Only Fred knows that."

Mary turned on the hazard lights so they wouldn't be hit from behind while they waited out the town moose, who seemed to be in no particular rush.

"However shall we pass the time?" Patrick asked, tipping his head for a better angle on the kiss.

Mary released her seat belt so she could get closer to him. "I've never made out in this car before."

She felt his smile against her lips and then let out a squeak of surprise when he pulled her over to rest on top of him. He did that with an ease that astounded her.

"You can't just haul me around like a sack of flour."

"Oh, but I can," he said, kissing her again.

"But—"

"Are we going to fight or make out?"

"Make out now. Fight later."

He groaned and kissed her with hours' worth of desire. Hiding how she felt about him at the wedding had been so difficult that it had almost been painful. She wanted the whole world to know that she loved this extraordinary man

151

and through some amazing stroke of fate, he loved her, too. But she'd never steal Hunter and Megan's thunder by choosing their moment to share her news.

No, it would keep for now.

Patrick came up for air and caressed her face, gazing at her with so much love that Mary might've swooned if she hadn't been reclined on top of him. "I'm so glad Cameron knows about us and that she's excited."

"Me, too."

"I'm looking forward to being able to tell everyone else our news."

The thought of it sent a quiver of excitement and dread through her.

"What's this?" he asked, his finger on the furrow that formed between her brows.

"You know I'm thrilled to be engaged to you and planning a life together, right?"

"I think so. I *hope* so."

"I am, Patrick. I swear."

"But?"

"I have some concerns, too."

"We should talk about them so I can make them go away. I don't want you worried about anything." Reaching around her, he laid on the horn.

Fred "mooed" in response.

"Is he for real?"

"He's large and in charge around here."

Patrick rolled down the window, letting in a blast of frigid air and snowflakes. "Come on, Fred. Be a pal. My lady and I just got engaged today, and we have a lot to talk about. Plans to be made, love to be made, things to do."

Mary rocked with silent laughter.

"Could you move your ass so we can go home? *Please?*"

After another deep "moo" that made Patrick jolt again,

Fred took a step forward and then another, shooting them a look that conveyed a world of annoyance for being disturbed.

"Thank Christ," Patrick said, pressing the button to close the window. He put Mary back in her seat as easily as he'd retrieved her.

"Knock that off!" she said indignantly.

"Never." He pressed the accelerator and got them home fifteen slow-going minutes later. "I've always hated driving in snow, but driving in snow with a moose on the loose is now my least-favorite activity."

"Come on," she said. "That was fun *and* funny."

"It was neither fun nor funny."

"You're funny when you're indignant."

"See what happens when I put a ring on her finger?" he asked when they were on the sidewalk that led to her front door. "She becomes mean and makes fun of me."

Mary gave him a little push from behind that sent him flying into a pile of snow left over from a storm two days earlier. Once again, she lost it laughing.

"Oh my God! You're so going to pay for that."

"I'm so sorry," she said between gasps of helpless laughter. She reached out a hand to help him up, and he gave it a tug that had her landing next to him, face-first in the snow.

She came up sputtering. "I can't believe you did that!"

He cracked up laughing. "Who's indignant now?"

She gathered up a handful of snow and mashed it into his face. "Who said, 'All's fair in love and checkers'?"

"This is war!" They wrestled in the snow, smashing it into faces and stuffing it down shirts, screaming with laughter and outrage.

Next door, an outside light came on, and they froze, like two children getting caught outside after bedtime.

"Hurry." Mary jumped up. "Let's get inside before Mrs.

Andersen comes out here to give us the third degree. She's the biggest gossip in town."

He got up and brushed the snow off his clothes. "So if I tell her we're engaged, the whole town will know by morning?"

"Yes," Mary hissed. "Now come on!" She grabbed his hand and tugged him along with her, getting them inside before Mrs. Andersen could come out to get the scoop of the year.

Inside, they removed their wet clothes and hung them up to dry, and then Patrick lit the fire.

"I might be getting too old to roll around in the snow," he said.

"You are going to be a grandfather soon. You probably ought to start acting like one."

"I'm seeing a whole new side to my Sweet Mary tonight," he said.

Smiling, she went to join him by the fire, wrapping her arms around him from behind. "I'm very sorry I laughed at you and pushed you into the snow. Believe it or not, neither was intentional."

"So you say."

"I mean it!"

He tugged on her hand, bringing her around him and into his arms. "I have more fun with you than I've had with anyone since I lost my wife."

She raised her hand to his face. "You make me laugh so hard."

"Am I facing a lifetime of you laughing at me?"

"I'll laugh *with* you more than *at* you."

Smiling, he kissed her. "I want you to put your ring back on."

"I'll go get it." She kissed him again and then got up to retrieve the ring she'd placed in a jewelry box before they left for the wedding, sliding it back on her finger and gazing at it with a feeling of incredulity that she was *engaged* to marry Patrick. The last few months had felt like a real-life fairy tale, and sometimes she still couldn't believe that this was now her life.

While she was in her bedroom, she also changed into the sexy black silk lingerie he'd sent her during the days of daily gifts.

A few weeks ago, she might've felt self-conscious about wearing something so sexy, but now she only felt excited for tonight and every night to come with him. The nightgown clung to her body, and the thong felt weird between her cheeks, but she suspected it wouldn't be on her for long. She topped off the outfit with scented body lotion and then brushed her hair and teeth.

When she returned to the living room, Patrick had removed his shirt and was reclined on the floor in front of the fire. He glanced up at her, and she would never, for the rest of her life, forget the expression on his face when he saw what she was wearing.

He rose to his knees and held out a hand to her.

Feeling giddy and happy, she took his outstretched hand and joined him on her knees in front of the fire.

"You are so incredibly beautiful all the time, but tonight..." He kissed her neck and wrapped his arms around her. "Tonight, you take my breath away." For the longest time, they stayed right there, on their knees, wrapped up in each other. Then he took hold of her left hand and kissed the back of it. "I love seeing you wearing my ring."

"I love wearing it."

"But you have concerns that we need to deal with."

"We can talk about that tomorrow."

He shook his head. "I don't want you to spend even one night worrying about anything. Talk to me." He brought her down to rest beside him next to the fire and pulled a blanket from the sofa to cover them.

Mary tried to think about what she wanted to say and the best way to put it. "I'd like to keep my house here."

"Of course, we will. We'll need a place to stay when we come to visit."

"I don't quite own it yet, but I will in another year or two—"

He rested a finger on her lips. "Mary, sweetheart. You're going to be my wife. We'll pay off the mortgage, and you'll own it free and clear. Please don't worry about things like that."

"I do worry about things like that, and things like money and how we're going to keep you from thinking you can spoil me rotten. I don't want that, and I don't want to be a trophy wife. I want to be productive." She paused, astounded to see his lips quivering. "Are you *laughing* at *me* now?"

"It was the trophy wife thing," he said, clearing his throat and making an obvious effort to contain his amusement. "Sorry, as you were saying…"

Mary poked him in the belly. "I'm being serious."

"I know you are, and I appreciate the sentiment of what you're saying. I've spoken to my personal attorney about several options—"

"Involving *me*?"

"Yes, involving you. I knew I was going to propose, and I was hopeful you'd say yes, so I've had a few conversations."

"What about?"

"He's adamant about a prenup, but I'm not interested in that."

"I want that. You have to protect yourself and your assets. You've worked so hard."

"I need to protect my assets from *you*?" he asked with that spark of amusement again.

"You know what I mean. I'm not after your assets. I love *you*, not your money."

He combed his fingers through her hair. "You have no idea how much that means to me, and that's exactly why I'm not interested in talking about a prenup. But I am interested in protecting both of us from any possible scenarios that neither of us wants to talk about. I'll be establishing an account in your name that will be yours to do with as you please. In addition to that, you'll have credit cards, health insurance, an automobile of your choice and anything else you need to feel safe and secure in our marriage. Those things are nonnegotiable for me."

"You're very generous, but I don't need a big account or a car—"

"Mary, honey, I understand that this is going to be a big change in lifestyle for you, but you can't ask me to become someone else entirely after we're married. I have a lot of money. I'll want to share that with you as we build a life together, and you have to let me take care of you. You're going to be my wife, my family. I need this, Mary."

She thought about what he'd said and then looked up at him. "I'll allow it within reason. I'd always rather you give money to the needy than shower me with diamonds and other things I don't need."

"I'm glad you mentioned charitable giving. I have a foundation that oversees my philanthropy. I'm sure there're any number of things you might be able to do to contribute to that effort. You can have full access to the business and the foundation and contribute anywhere that interests you."

Mary's brows lifted. "*Full* access?"

Kissing her, he said, "Full and complete access to my life. Whatever you want is what I want. But I don't want you to be so busy and overcommitted that you can't jump on the plane with me when I have to go here, there or everywhere."

"Is this really happening, or have I dreamed this entire thing?"

"You, my Sweet Mary from Vermont, are my dream come true, and I'm never going to let you go."

"I can live with that."

EPILOGUE

*M*ary broke the news to Linc that she was leaving the company on the Saturday morning after she and Patrick returned to Vermont from their romantic trip to Martinique to hear the news that Hannah and Nolan's baby had been born early. Mary called Linc to give him her two-week notice with tears streaming down her face as she told him her life had taken an unexpected change in direction.

He'd replied with stunned silence.

"Linc? Are you there?"

"I'm here. I'm just… I… What'll we do without you, Mary?"

"Oh, stop. You'll be fine. You'll find someone great to take my place."

"No one can replace you."

"Linc… I'm sorry. I'm…"

"Please don't be sorry. Just tell me you're happy about this new direction."

"I'm very happy, and I'll tell you all about it when I see

you on Monday. I wanted to call you because I knew there'd be ugly tears, and I didn't want to do that in front of you."

He laughed. "You may be surprised to hear there're a few tears on my end as well."

"I'll never have the words to tell you what you, your family, the company and this job have meant to me."

"You are part of our family, Mary. You always will be."

"Thank you. Thank you so much for everything and for understanding."

"I'm looking forward to hearing about what's next for you."

"I'm looking forward to telling you. I'd like to tell everyone at the same time, if that's all right with you. I don't have enough tears to do this one at a time."

"I'll call a family meeting for Monday morning, and you can share your news with all of us."

"Okay, that sounds good. I'll see you then."

Mary fell into Patrick's outstretched arms, sobbing from the emotional wallop of making the call that would put their plans into motion.

"There now, honey," he said, stroking her hair, "it's okay. Everything will be okay."

"I know," she said, hiccupping. "It was just hard to tell him."

"I'm going to stay for that meeting on Monday."

"But you have to get back to work."

"One more day won't hurt anything. I want to be with you when you tell them our news."

"So you're not leaving tomorrow?"

"I'm not leaving tomorrow."

More tears slid down her cheeks, which he brushed away with light strokes of his fingertips. "I thought that would make you happy."

"I'm so happy."

Patrick laughed and hugged her close. "That's all that matters."

HE CAME WITH HER TO WORK ON MONDAY MORNING WHERE the entire Abbott tribe had gathered to hear her big news. They took one look at her holding Patrick's hand, and Charley said, "Pay up, everyone! I told you it was him!"

"You took *bets*?" Mary asked, astounded.

"Of course we did," Charley said. "Have you met us?"

Mary laughed at her predictably saucy comment.

"We've known for weeks!" Cameron said, raising her hands and doing a little dance.

"Since when?" Hunter asked. Just back from his honeymoon to Bermuda, he was tanned and as relaxed looking as Mary had ever seen the tightly wound CFO and eldest Abbott sibling.

"Since the night of your wedding," Cameron said, sticking her tongue out at her brother-in-law.

"I can't believe you guys kept such a big secret," Ella said. "That's very un-Abbott-like of you."

"No kidding," Lucas Abbott said. "We suck at secrets."

"Um, I knew, too," Molly said sheepishly.

Everyone stared at her, especially her husband. "You knew they were together and didn't tell me?"

"I'm sorry, honey, but you're a terrible gossip, and they weren't ready for everyone to know."

"I am *not* a gossip," Lincoln said to howls of laughter from his family.

"Whatever you say, Dad," Charley said.

"Gotta side with the kids on this one, Linc," his father-in-law, Elmer, said.

"You're one to talk, Gramps," Colton said.

"I have no idea what you mean."

"Sure, you don't."

Elmer hugged and kissed Mary and shook Patrick's hand. "I hope you'll both be very happy."

"So I guess there's no need for any kind of announcement, then," Patrick said, seeming overwhelmed by the Abbott family dynamics. They were still in the foyer, and the cat was already out of the bag.

"Well, we do still have one additional thing to share," Mary said, extending her hand so they could see her ring.

While everyone exclaimed over the beautiful ring and congratulated the happy couple, Charley said, "Who had engaged in the betting?"

"That'd be me," Max Abbott said, grinning as he held Caden in his arms.

"Crap," Charley said. "That makes you the big winner. Five hundred bucks."

"These people don't mess around, do they?" Patrick asked.

"You have no idea," Mary said, patting his arm as she took in the chaos with a bittersweet feeling. She'd miss them all so much. Thank goodness Patrick's daughter lived here so they'd have an excuse to frequently return to visit.

"Congratulations, dear friends," Molly said, hugging Mary and then Patrick. "I'm so happy for both of you."

"Thank you so much, Molly," Mary said, returning her embrace. "For your advice and for not telling Linc before we were ready."

"I still can't believe you kept this from me," Linc said to his wife, a playful glower directed her way.

"She did what I asked her to," Mary said. "We weren't ready for people to know yet. I just hope you can find someone to take good care of you all after I'm gone."

"About that," Colton's fiancée, Lucy, said, grinning widely. "I hear my sister and niece might be moving to Butler to come to work for the family business."

"Oh," Mary said, clapping her hands. "Emma! How perfect! You must be so excited, Lucy."

"I still can't believe it," Lucy said. "And she talked my dad into coming with them. Everyone I love in one place."

"That makes me so happy," Mary said. "I feel so much better about leaving knowing you'll be in such good hands."

Patrick slipped his arms around her from behind. "And so will you, my love."

BONUS EPILOGUE

"So," Elmer said over coffee at the diner, "Mary and Patrick are engaged. How about them apples?"

"I like them apples," Linc said. "He's been alone for thirty years, and if anyone deserves a second chance at love, it's him. And Mary…" Linc shook his head. "I love her like a sister. I'm going to miss her so much, but I couldn't be happier for the two of them."

"They'll be back to visit a lot, especially now that there's going to be a grandchild in the mix."

"True."

"Are you worried about Cam? Because of what happened to her mother?"

"I actually talked to Will about it, and you won't believe it. Before they even tried for a baby, she spent two nights at Mass General to make sure there was no reason she shouldn't have kids."

"And?" Elmer asked.

"All clear."

"Well, that's a huge relief."

"Indeed. Molly and I were so proud of them for taking such a proactive step."

"They're good kids, and they'll be great parents."

"Yes, they will. We're in the midst of what could be the biggest baby boom in recorded history."

"You're the one who had ten kids," Elmer said with a huff of laughter.

"Speaking of my ten kids, have you heard any more about the situation with Mia, the woman Wade is interested in?"

"Formal charges were filed last week against the people arrested in the drug bust."

"Mia wasn't charged with anything, was she?"

Elmer shook his head. "From what I can tell, she wasn't involved, but I can't help but wonder what she knows."

"This whole thing makes me very nervous. I don't want my son anywhere near this crap."

"Understood, but I wonder… Do you suppose he knows that everyone around her was scooped up in this big bust and that she might be *available*?"

Linc pondered that for a long moment. "What're you suggesting?"

"I'd like to have a conversation with him. Feel him out. See what he knows—and what he *doesn't*. What do you think?"

"I don't know. My better judgment is telling me to stay away from this. It's got trouble written all over it."

"If you could've heard the way he talked about her, you'd be singing a different tune. He's crazy about her, and this could be the perfect opportunity for him to step up for her in a time of need."

"What if it turns out she was involved in the same stuff her friends were?"

"Wade's no fool. If that's the case, he won't go near her. He's such a health nut that he wouldn't have anything to do with drugs or anyone who was involved in dealing them. You know that."

"Still… Love makes people do crazy things."

"Our Wade Abbott will never be crazy enough to get anywhere near drug dealing, love or no love."

"You make a good point." Linc released a deep sigh. "Okay. You can talk to him and see what he knows."

Elmer rubbed his hands together gleefully. "I'll get right on that. And PS, if it works out between them, this one is *all* mine."

"How did I know you were going to say that?"

THANK YOU FOR READING *CAN'T BUY ME LOVE*! I'VE BEEN SO looking forward to writing Patrick and Mary's story ever since they met in *You'll Be Mine*. I hope you enjoyed reading it as much as I loved writing it. I like to see some of the more "mature" members of the cast get their happy ending. After you finish reading, make sure you join the Can't Buy Me Love Reader Group at *https://www.facebook.com/groups/Cant-BuyMeLoveReaders/* to chat with other readers about Patrick and Mary's story.

Here Comes the Sun, the next book in the Butler Series, will feature Wade Abbott's long-awaited story. Keep reading for more information.

As always, thank you to my behind-the-scenes team that makes it possible to keep the books coming so quickly—Julie Cupp, Lisa Cafferty, Holly Sullivan, Isabel Sullivan, Nikki Colquhoun, Cheryl Serra, Ashley Lopez and Courtney Lopes. You ladies are the best, and I appreciate you all so much.

Thanks to my editing team of Linda Ingmanson and Joyce Lamb, and my beta readers, Anne Woodall, Kara

Conrad and Holly Sullivan, for helping me to produce clean, well-edited books.

Biggest thanks of all to my readers, whose support makes everything possible. I'm so grateful to every one of you!

xoxo

Marie

Coming up next in the Butler, Vermont Series, Wade and Mia's story, *Here Comes the Sun!* Turn the page for a sneak peek.

HERE COMES THE SUN

Chapter 1

"I love those who yearn for the impossible." —Johann Wolfgang von Goethe

Even with snow swirling around him, Wade Abbott knew the way home. He could find it blindfolded, which he was basically doing since the whiteout snow made it so he had to rely on everything but his vision. He'd been out with his brothers for hours looking for two young boys who'd gone sledding in the foothills of Butler Mountain and disappeared in the blizzard.

They'd found them alive but hypothermic forty-five minutes ago and dispersed to head home to warm up. His younger brothers, Lucas and Landon, both paramedics, had transported the boys to the hospital, where they'd be reunited with their grateful parents.

The snowmobile's headlight illuminated the Nelsons' mailbox, a green monstrosity that indicated Wade was about five hundred feet from his own driveway. He noticed a pattern in the snow that looked an awful lot like footprints. Who would be foolish enough to be out in a full-on blizzard if they didn't have to be?

Was he hallucinating, or were the footprints leading to his place? A trickle of unease traveled down his back, which was odd because he never felt unsafe in Butler, Vermont. Hell, he never even locked his door. He didn't have to. His place wasn't easy to find unless you knew where it was.

He hung a right into his driveway and followed the deep footsteps for a quarter mile of twists and bends until his cabin came into view, nestled into a copse of evergreens, his own piece of paradise.

Biting one of the fingers of his glove, he pulled it off and reached for the flashlight strapped to his hip to further illuminate the yard. The flashlight's beam cut through the snow to identify a huddled lump on his porch.

"What the hell?" Wade cut the engine and jumped off the snowmobile. Fighting the foot-high snow, he crossed the yard and went up the stairs. "Hello?"

Nothing.

He nudged the lump with his foot.

It moaned.

He scooped up the bundle and carried it inside, where heat from the woodstove he'd stoked earlier swept over him. Dropping to his knees in front of the fire, he deposited his visitor.

She moaned again.

Dear God, it's a woman—a half-frozen woman. Moving quickly, he threw two more logs on the fire and began unwrapping the ice-crusted scarf that covered her face so the heat could penetrate. Bruises. Her face was black, blue and swollen, so much so he didn't immediately recognize her.

And then he knew.

His heart skipped a beat and shock reverberated through

him as he began to frantically remove her wet coat and gloves.

"Mia." He could hear the panic in his own voice. *"Mia!"*

She moaned again. Her lips and fingers were blue.

Wade rubbed her hands between his. "Mia, talk to me." What was she doing here, and who had beat the hell out of her? Rage simmered in his gut. He'd suspected from when he first met her almost two years ago at a yoga retreat that the man in her life— Wade assumed it was her husband—was hurting her, but they'd never reached the point where he felt comfortable asking her about it. Throughout their friendship, he'd seen the signs: skittish, jumpy, secretive, scared, but she hadn't shared anything overly personal with him.

She'd broken off contact with him a year ago, and he'd suffered ever since, wondering why she'd stopped calling him and worrying whether she was safe.

"Mia, honey... Wake up. Please wake up." He would've called for help if anyone could've gotten to them in the storm. Since outside help wasn't an option tonight, it was up to him to get her warm. Unzipping his parka, he pulled it off, removed his boots, kicked them aside and then took off the survival suit that allowed him to be out in a storm for hours without suffering hypothermia. He stripped down to underwear so he could use his body heat to warm her.

Then he went to work on her clothing, moving carefully in case she had other injuries. Working from her boots up, he took off soaking-wet clothes that had him wondering just how long she'd been out in the storm.

Other than the violent tremors that rattled her body, she never stirred as he stripped her down to panties and a tank top, both of which were damp. He laid her wet clothes on top of the woodstove to dry and then stopped short at the sight of arms and legs mottled with bruises of various colors.

Wade choked back the rage that burned through him. He

blew out a deep breath, grabbed a down comforter from the sofa and pulled it over them as he molded his body to hers, hoping his body heat would help to raise her core temperature. It would be better, he knew from his lifesaving training, if they were both bare, but he didn't think he could handle that.

Hopefully, he could get her warm without having to strip down completely.

He was enveloped in the sweet, fresh scent of her hair, while his heart beat erratically, his palms felt sweaty despite the cold and his mind raced. What had brought her here? Who had hurt her? What did she want from him? Could he bear to see her again and then watch her go back to wherever she'd been the last year? He tightened his hold on her. He wouldn't let her go back to the man who'd been hurting her, that much he knew for certain.

"Mia, honey, you're safe. It's Wade. I'm so glad you're here. We're going to get you warm." He ran his hand gently up and down her arm, wishing she would wake up and talk to him. He'd missed her so much. Talking to her had once been his favorite thing. After they first met at the yoga retreat, they'd connected a few times at coffee shops between his home in Butler and hers in Rutland. He'd driven more than an hour each way for the chance to spend thirty minutes in her presence.

The last time he'd heard from her, she'd told him she couldn't talk to him anymore. He'd begged her to reconsider and promised to keep his distance so as not to cause her any further difficulty. But he hadn't heard from her again, until he found her on his doorstep, nearly frozen and obviously injured.

Her poor face was so terribly swollen that it made his heart hurt to look at her.

God… He'd gladly kill the man who'd done this to her, and he had no doubt it'd been a man.

He pressed his lips to her forehead. "Sweetheart, wake up and talk to me. It's Wade. It's okay now. No one will ever hurt you again."

The only reply he got was a tortured-sounding moan.

"Mia."

Her lids fluttered open, revealing the gorgeous navy-blue eyes that had once looked at him with such affection. She stared at him, almost as if she couldn't believe her eyes. "Wade," she whispered.

"It's me, honey. You're safe with me."

She began to cry.

Her tears broke him. "Shhh, it's okay. Everything is okay now."

She shook her head as her teeth chattered. "N-no, it isn't."

"It is for right now. The only thing you need to worry about is getting warm. Hold on to me and let me warm you up."

Mia burrowed deeper into his embrace, her arm sliding around his waist and her leg slipping between his.

Wade swallowed hard. Here in his arms was the woman he'd dreamed about since the day he met her. He was supposed to be helping her get warm, but her nearness was making him hot in more ways than one. He took a deep breath and scooted his hips back a crucial inch so she wouldn't be able to feel what her nearness had done to him.

What did it mean that she'd come to him? He'd once written down his home address and phone number as well as the address and phone number for the office and told her to use the info if she ever needed him for anything at any time. With cell phone service nonexistent in Butler, he didn't own a mobile phone, so he'd given her all the other ways to reach him. After so much time, he figured she'd thrown away the scrap of paper and forgotten about him.

He had never forgotten her. Thoughts of her and what she might be going through had tormented him through months of sleepless nights and long days at work in which he'd moved through his life in a perpetual state of despair. He'd known Mia a year when he first shared his complex feelings for her with his sister Hannah. His sister Ella knew about her, too, and he'd told his grandfather a little about her, but he hadn't told anyone else, preferring to keep his feelings—and his despair—to himself.

As one of ten kids, most of whom worked together running the family's Green Mountain Country Store, it wasn't easy to keep secrets in his family. But he'd been aided by the fact that he was considered the "quiet" one of the bunch. No one thought much of it when Wade sat back and took in the madness of their family rather than actively participating. So he'd been able to keep his situation relatively private, which, in his family, was saying something.

He had so many questions for her—especially why now and what now—but he didn't ask any of them. Rather, he stayed focused on warming her and containing the desire zipping through his body, a reminder of how much he'd wanted her from the first time he laid eyes on her.

For a long time after Wade settled them in front of the fire, Mia shivered so hard, her teeth ached. She'd never been so cold in her life. Her car had gotten stuck in a snowdrift on the outskirts of Butler. Fortunately, she'd spent hours studying road maps into and out of Butler. In the back of her mind every second of the last miserable year had been Wade's address, the phone numbers she'd memorized, along with the map of Butler that had represented her path to freedom.

Her biggest concern as she'd plotted her escape was that Wade might not be willing to help her. She'd had to hope and pray that he would still want her the way he once had, even if he'd never said the words. A woman knew these things, and her life now depended upon him still feeling the same way.

He was so warm and solid as he caressed her back in small, soothing circles that made her want to purr with pleasure. She had no idea how long they lay cuddled up to each other under the heavenly blanket, but after a while, her teeth stopped chattering and sensation returned to her extremities in painful pricks. The warmth flooded her mind and body, filling her with a sense of security that was even more blissful than the heat coming from the woodstove—and his muscular body.

For so long, she'd had to wonder what it might be like to be touched by Wade Abbott, and now she knew what heaven must be like. She took deep breaths of the woodsy, natural scent of him and noted that he'd cut his hair since she'd last seen him. Once upon a time, she'd sat across from him in coffee shops and wished she could run her fingers over the sharp planes of his face and touch the longish hair that wasn't brown or blond or red, but rather, an interesting golden mix of all three colors.

During those visits, she'd memorized every detail, right down to the flecks of gold in his eyes that glittered with pleasure whenever he looked at her while they talked until their coffee grew cold and the sun dipped toward the horizon.

Every time she'd left him, she'd done so under a veil of panic, certain this would be the time her secret friendship with Wade would be discovered by a man who would kill her before he'd let anyone else have her. But somehow, they'd gotten away with it. Other things had transpired that'd convinced her to stay away from Wade, for his safety as much as hers, but she'd never stopped thinking about him, wondering about him or wishing that things were different.

Had he thought about her, too? Or had he moved on with someone else? Was there a woman sleeping in his bedroom at this very moment? Would he hold her this way if he had someone else? If it meant saving her life, she knew for sure he would. But once her body was warm, would he leave her to join the woman he loved?

That was like a knife to her heart. Thoughts of him had kept her alive long before tonight, and all her hopes were pinned on him being willing to help her now. She wiggled even closer to him and encountered evidence that he wanted her as much as he always had.

He gasped as she rubbed against him. "Mia…"

The proof of his desire freed her to ask for what she wanted more than anything. "Will you kiss me, Wade?"

He stared at her, seeming incredulous. "Are you really here asking me to kiss you? Will I wake up tomorrow to find out I dreamed this?"

She placed her hand on his face because she'd wanted to for so long and now she could. "It's not a dream. I'm really here, and I've been dying for your kiss for as long as I've known you."

Closing his eyes, he took a deep breath and released it before opening them again. "What about your husband?"

"I don't have a husband."

A strangled sound escaped his tightly clenched jaw in the second before his lips found hers with the light of the fire and years of yearning to guide them. "I don't want to hurt you."

"I'm okay, and I really want you to kiss me."

He kissed her like a man possessed. His fingers dug into her hair and shaped her skull, making it impossible for her to escape, not that she had any wish to be anywhere but right there with him. She'd waited what felt like forever for him to kiss her, and the reality was a thousand times better than the fantasies had ever been.

To call this a kiss didn't do justice to the feelings that exploded inside her as his tongue found hers in an erotic, sensual dance that made her dizzy and weak with longing.

"Mia…" He withdrew slowly, gently kissing the uninjured side of her face, jaw and neck. "You have no idea how long I've wanted to kiss you."

"Don't stop." She sounded desperate and wanton but couldn't be bothered to care. Combing her fingers through his hair, she brought him back for more.

They kissed like they were afraid this was all they'd ever have. Perhaps it was. Perhaps he wouldn't be able to help her, and if that were the case, she'd have no choice but to leave him. For his sake, as well as hers, it would have to be all or nothing.

One kiss became two and then three, and when they came up for air, he was pressed up against her, and she wasn't cold anymore. Not even kind of.

He gazed at her, the firelight turning his hair and skin to pure gold. "Who hurt you, Mia?"

"The man I used to love."

"Why would he do this to you?" He ran his fingertips gently over the bruise on her left cheek.

"That's a very long story."

"You can't go back to him," he said fiercely. "I *knew* he was hurting you, but I couldn't prove it, and you'd never talk to me about him."

"Because I couldn't."

"How did you get here?"

"I drove as far as I could, but my car got stuck in a drift on the way into town. I walked the rest of the way."

"That's *miles* from here!"

"I don't know how far it was, but it took a long time, and then when I got here and you weren't home... The last thing I remember is reaching for the door hoping you wouldn't mind."

"I wouldn't have. Of course you could've come in."

"I must've passed out before I made up my mind."

"My place isn't easy to find. You'd have to know where it is to find it, especially in this weather."

"After you gave me your address, I looked it up on a map, and I memorized the route."

"*Why*, Mia? Why did you memorize the way to my home?"

"Because I knew I'd come to you as soon as I could. I only hoped that I'd still be welcome after all this time."

"You're always welcome with me. You know that." He looked at her with love and joy and hope. So much hope that her heart contracted. "You still haven't told me what happened or why you came tonight, in the middle of a blizzard."

"Because..." She swallowed hard, summoning the fortitude she needed to say the words. "I need you to do something for me."

"I'd do anything for you."

His fierce words made her want to weep from the relief of knowing she hadn't misjudged him or his feelings for her.

"Tell me what you need, Mia. There's nothing you could ask of me that would be too much."

Looking up to meet his intense brown-eyed gaze, she said, "I need you to marry me."

Here Comes the Sun is available in print from Amazon.com and other online retailers, or you can purchase a signed copy from Marie's store at shop.marieforce.com.

Book 5: Hoping for Love (*Evan & Grace*)

Book 6: Season for Love (*Owen & Laura*)

Book 7: Longing for Love (*Blaine & Tiffany*)

Book 8: Waiting for Love (*Adam & Abby*)

Book 9: Time for Love (*David & Daisy*)

Book 10: Meant for Love (*Jenny & Alex*)

Book 10.5: Chance for Love, *A Gansett Island Novella* (*Jared & Lizzie*)

Book 11: Gansett After Dark (*Owen & Laura*)

Book 12: Kisses After Dark (*Shane & Katie*)

Book 13: Love After Dark (*Paul & Hope*)

Book 14: Celebration After Dark (*Big Mac & Linda*)

Book 15: Desire After Dark (*Slim & Erin*)

Book 16: Light After Dark (*Mallory & Quinn*)

Book 17: Victoria & Shannon (Episode 1)

Book 18: Kevin & Chelsea (Episode 2)

A Gansett Island Christmas Novella

Book 19: Mine After Dark (*Riley & Nikki*)

Book 20: Yours After Dark (*Finn & Chloe*)

Book 21: Trouble After Dark (*Deacon & Julia*)

Book 22: Rescue After Dark (*Mason & Jordan*)

Book 23: Blackout After Dark

The Treading Water Series
Book 1: Treading Water

Book 2: Marking Time

Book 3: Starting Over

Book 4: Coming Home

Book 5: Finding Forever

The Miami Nights Series

Book 1: How Much I Feel *(Carmen & Jason)*

Book 2: How Much I Care *(Maria & Austin)*

Book 3: How Much I Love *(Dee's story)*

Single Titles

Five Years Gone

One Year Home

Sex Machine

Sex God

Georgia on My Mind

True North

The Fall

The Wreck

Love at First Flight

Everyone Loves a Hero

Line of Scrimmage

The Quantum Series

Book 1: Virtuous *(Flynn & Natalie)*

Book 2: Valorous *(Flynn & Natalie)*

Book 3: Victorious *(Flynn & Natalie)*

Book 4: Rapturous *(Addie & Hayden)*

Book 5: Ravenous *(Jasper & Ellie)*

Book 6: Delirious *(Kristian & Aileen)*

Book 7: Outrageous *(Emmett & Leah)*

Book 8: Famous *(Marlowe & Sebastian)*

Romantic Suspense Novels Available from Marie Force

The Fatal Series

One Night With You, *A Fatal Series Prequel Novella*

Book 1: Fatal Affair

Book 2: Fatal Justice

Book 3: Fatal Consequences

Book 3.5: Fatal Destiny, *the Wedding Novella*

Book 4: Fatal Flaw

Book 5: Fatal Deception

Book 6: Fatal Mistake

Book 7: Fatal Jeopardy

Book 8: Fatal Scandal

Book 9: Fatal Frenzy

Book 10: Fatal Identity

Book 11: Fatal Threat

Book 12: Fatal Chaos

Book 13: Fatal Invasion

Book 14: Fatal Reckoning

Book 15: Fatal Accusation

Book 16: Fatal Fraud

Historical Romance Available from Marie Force

The Gilded Series

Book 1: Duchess by Deception

Book 2: Deceived by Desire

ABOUT THE AUTHOR

Marie Force is the *New York Times*
bestselling author of contemporary
romance, romantic suspense and erotic
romance. Her series include Gansett
Island, Fatal, Treading Water, Butler
Vermont and Quantum.

Her books have sold nearly 10 million copies worldwide,
have been translated into more than a dozen languages and
have appeared on the *New York Times* bestseller more than 30
times. She is also a *USA Today* and *Wall Street Journal* bestseller, as well as a Speigel bestseller in Germany.

Her goals in life are simple—to finish raising two happy,
healthy, productive young adults, to keep writing books for
as long as she possibly can and to never be on a flight that
makes the news.

Join Marie's mailing list on her website at *marieforce.com*
for news about new books and upcoming appearances in
your area. Follow her on Facebook at *www.Facebook.-
com/MarieForceAuthor* and on Instagram at *www.instagram.-
com/marieforceauthor/*. Contact Marie at
marie@marieforce.com.

CPSIA information can be obtained
at www.ICGtesting.com
Printed in the USA
BVHW092159150722
642040BV00005B/332